BEATRICE
ON HER OWN

by Rosemary Zibart

Dedication

To the many young people in the world today who are trying to make the world a safer, healthier and kinder place.

CHAPTER ONE

"It won't be any fun," declared Arabella. She was gazing at herself in the mirror, admiring her red curls and critically regarding her somewhat chubby waist. "Dorothea has just invited girls." Since turning thirteen, my lively friend thought a birthday party that didn't include boys was bound to be boring.

"We can still dress up," I said, knowing that would please Arabella. "And there will be cake and ice cream."

Arabella's eyes sparkled. "Then I'm glad there won't be boys—we won't need to eat dainty 'lady-like' portions." She stuck up her nose and pranced around.

"Is that how you imagine *ladies* behave?" I asked.

"Well, I guess you'd know, Beatrice." When she used my full name, I knew she was mimicking my being so "upper-crust" British.

"Undoubtedly some ladies I've known were real snoots," I retorted, "but certainly not all."

"Not you at least." Arabella grinned. "Not any more."

I returned the grin. Then I took a turn in front of the mirror. In the past year I'd added an inch or two in height, without a single curve to soften the profile. Oh well…that'll come soon enough, Clem had assured me.

It was noon as we crossed the Santa Fe Plaza on our way to the party. The Plaza was one of the first places Arabella had shown me when I had arrived in this dusty little town over a year ago. At that time, its tall trees were crowned with golden leaves and the benches beneath filled with friendly people, reminding me of London's lovely parks before the war. Though in Santa Fe, you are just as likely to hear *"buenos dias"* as "hello" because it was a frontier outpost first of Spain and then Mexico for 300 years.

On this wintry day, the trees were bare and the short grass a dull brown. A chill wind lifted the remaining brown leaves, scattering them about. Despite the harsh weather, the Plaza was full of small groups of people, warmly wrapped, and speaking intently to one another. Across the Plaza, I spied our classmate Esteban and waved. On weekends he often worked there, shining shoes. Today he rushed up to us, his eyes wide and wild, a newspaper flapping in his hand.

"Look…look at this," he stammered.

I took the paper and stared at the headline. My stomach flipped. It couldn't be true. It just couldn't. I opened my mouth but felt too ill to speak.

Arabella grabbed the newspaper and read more closely. "Over a dozen American ships bombed." She looked up. "Where's Pearl Harbor?"

"On the island of Hawaii," said Esteban. "A territory of the

United States. That means the Japanese bombed *our* country."

"How awful," I murmured, almost choking on the words. "Bombs."

Arabella and Esteban swiftly turned in my direction and stared—as if I knew something they didn't. And they were right—I did know about bombs. Far too well.

In the weeks before fleeing London, I had huddled in underground shelters with my family. I had heard the terrifying whistle of bombs dropping from the sky and felt the earth around us violently shake as each exploded. I had crept outside, morning after morning, and seen the rubble and smelled the smoke. I had watched as bodies on stretchers were lifted into ambulances. Many times, I had squeezed Father's hand tightly and pressed my face into his soft camel's hair coat, unable to watch any longer.

Could it happen here?

"I don't want to go to the party." Arabella's face had lost its fresh pink. "I couldn't eat any cake."

"Don't worry, there won't be a party," I muttered. "Nobody will want to celebrate today."

"Sorry to give you the bad news." Esteban's eyes dwelled on me another second. "Damn Japs," he muttered. "We'll get 'em." A scowl I'd never seen before darkened his brow.

Then he crossed the Plaza to join a group of his buddies who were huddled under the naked sycamores. No one seemed to be doing anything that day except talking and talking.

Arabella and I left the Plaza, walking a little ways together. She babbled about something but I didn't catch a word. Then we separated and each headed home. Home is where you want to be when something dreadful happens. My stomach ached and I had a strange taste in my mouth. Was it fear?

When I reached home, Clem was seated in the living room, glued to the large radio in the corner. The lines on her sober face seemed deeper. As a nurse, she had witnessed war; she knew about "casualties" and the effort to keep wounded soldiers alive.

Seeing me, she looked relieved and made room on the sofa. "I guess you've heard?"

I nodded, then sank down next to her. Some of my panic abated. Clem was such a solid, sensible person, such a comfort.

Oh, how my present view of Clem had radically changed from my first!

At the train station when she arrived to pick me up, my heart nearly dropped to the soles of my patent leather pumps. Emerging from a dusty pickup in scuffed cowboy boots and shapeless trousers, she didn't resemble anyone I'd ever known. Certainly not my elegant mother and her fashionable friends. Clem was altogether different—a public health nurse who worked long hours at the nearby Indian pueblos and Spanish villages – she had little time to fuss with her clothes or hairdo.

Of course Clem certainly wasn't expecting *me* either, when she volunteered to host a child from Great Britain. "A little princess," she had observed with a grin. And I had to work hard to prove I was anything else.

That evening we remained close by the radio, eager for every dispatch. Twenty-one American ships had been sunk or badly damaged. Several thousand American soldiers killed.

Neither of us gave any thought to dinner and my stomach-ache increased by the hour. Finally, before dragging myself off to bed, I turned to Clem. "I feel horrible," I murmured.

"We all feel bad," she replied.

"But I feel especially horrid," I exclaimed. "Because all last year, I was hoping and praying the United States would join the war in order to help Britain. Now it will certainly join the fight." Tears ran down my cheeks. "My wish has come true—in the most awful way."

Clem put her arms around me. "Oh honey, it was natural for you to want the United States to become Great Britain's ally. England couldn't defeat its enemies without American help." She sighed. "War is terrible. Don't I know…" Her gaze wandered in the distance for a second. "But sometimes we don't have a choice. We have to fight. This is one of those times." She seemed loath to let me go, as if our tight hug was holding us both upright.

Her sad look remained with me later, as I climbed into bed. I could still hear patchy radio broadcasts. In homes across the country, I imagined, people were listening to news that didn't get any better as the night wore on.

Rolling over, I stared at the photograph of my family, my eyes brimming with tears. Then I reached under the bed. My fingers touched the flat wooden box where I preserved all my letters from home. Pulling it out, I chose one to read.

I May 1941

Dear Beatrice,

I know you wish to know all you can. But the news remains bleak. The bombing still goes on almost nightly. Your dear London is a veritable ghost town—so many people have fled to the countryside or to other countries, as you did. Yet we who remain stay busy and attempt to cheer up one another. We're all in the same bowl of soup, so to speak.

Driving for the Ambulance Corps, I must admit, can be a lark. Only last week, we plunged into a burning building and rescued an elderly woman as well as a pet poodle, a very upset Siamese cat, and a small green parakeet that had miraculously survived the smoke and fumes. People make such a fuss about their pets! But animals are especially dear, I believe, when a person has lost her home and nearly everything in it!

Despite the heavy bombing, there are a few incorrigibles, like our dear Great-Aunt Augusta who simply refuses to leave the city. She won't even alter her afternoon tea time. "If the Nazis compel us to change our habits," she declares, "they've practically won the war."

Instead of going to an underground station during bombing raids as we're all requested to do, she instructed Harris, the butler, and Hadley, the chauffeur, to put that massive ugly dining room table in the lowest room in the house. Then a feather mattress and pillow were placed underneath.

A week ago, all of them—Harris, Hadley, and Annie, the scullery maid – hadn't time to flee elsewhere so they joined Great-Aunt Augusta on the mattress beneath the table. To her credit, I heard she didn't complain a bit, though with their combined girths, it must have been a tight fit.

My own most desperate experience occurred on a lovely Saturday afternoon when Father and I were driving out to Dorset to visit Mother who's now staying there full time with Aunt Elizabeth. The sky was as deep blue as those you describe in New Mexico. We had paused at a turn-about in the road. Suddenly, with a deafening roar, a German spitfire appeared from nowhere, swooping down and blistering the ground with machine gun bullets.

Father and I had just enough time to scramble out of the automobile and dive underneath. Minutes later, we both emerged dusty but unscathed. In fact, we were laughing about our good luck when we spied a poor fellow. He'd taken refuge in a nearby telephone booth—but now he was covered with shattered glass, quite bloody and dead. Both Father and I just stood there too shocked to move for several moments. Though glad to be alive, we were horrified by the man's terrible ending.

I hope this nasty account doesn't give you nightmares. I just want to assure you again that you're so much better off 5,000 miles away from this beastly war!!

Your best and only brother,
William James Sims III

With trembling fingers I re-inserted the letter into the envelope and returned it to the box under the bed. I had received this unsettling bit of news almost six months ago. May was the last month of the heavy bombing in London, thank goodness. But, sadly enough, that was also one of the last *real* letters Willy wrote. A few weeks later, he turned eighteen and graduated from serving in the Home Guard to serving in the Royal Air Force. Mother was desolate. Now neither she nor I received more than a hasty note that Willy has penned between his airman duties.

Indeed, my family had been thrilled I was so far from the war. How would they feel now that the war was no longer distant? When it had suddenly arrived on our doorstep? As Willy would say: *Now we're all in the soup together!*

CHAPTER TWO

Next morning I could barely unstick my eyelids from my cheeks. But it was Monday, a school day. Would there be school? I threw on some clothes and hurried downstairs. The housekeeper, Dolores, was in the kitchen cooking eggs and tortillas, as usual. When I walked in, she was bent over the stove.

"*Buenos dias.* Do you know if there's–"

Without responding, Dolores rushed over and hugged me. "*Mi'jita, mi'jita.*" Her eyes were red-rimmed and teary.

"Yes, there's school." Esteban, my school chum, was also Dolores' son. He sat at the kitchen table, his shoulders tightly hunched, studying the newspaper. "You know how many New Mexican soldiers are over there??"

"In Hawaii?"

"The Philippines," he mumbled, finally looking up. "My cousins, Ricardo and Manuel, are there." He shook his head. "And probably a few other cousins we don't know about."

He pushed the newspaper toward me. The headline

was huge: MANILA BOMBED. Manila was the capital of the Philippines. And then I remembered: The New Mexico Artillery had been posted to that region months ago. The battalion was considered one of the finest in the army—best sharpshooters in uniform. Plus, most people from the Philippines (Filipinos) spoke Spanish, and so did many New Mexicans. The U.S. Army must have considered it a perfect fit.

I gasped. "The Philippines are near Japan."

Esteban nodded. "Very near."

"We must pray for their safety, *jito*," said Dolores. She looked as if she'd aged several years in a day.

Scanning the front page, I spied a report of Japanese aircraft carriers in the Pacific Ocean off the United States coast. "We fear an attack on Los Angeles any hour, any day," declared the governor of California. According to another article, New Mexico's state and local police had been put on a full emergency alert.

I plunked down in a seat at the kitchen table. Usually the scene of lively chatter, the room was strangely silent. All of us dwelling on the darkest of thoughts. The war had engulfed nearly the entire world. First, Europe—a disaster I'd witnessed myself. And then from what I'd learned from newspaper and radio accounts—how the war had crept into Asia and North Africa. Now it was reaching its brutal fingers across the globe to sunny Santa Fe, squeezing the heart of our happy little town.

Normally, when Esteban and I walked to school together, we joked and teased the whole way. Arabella accused me of "flirting"—one of her nonsensical notions. Still, I prayed no one else had noticed how this handsome dark-haired lad always caused a tiny smile to glow on my lips.

That Monday, however, we walked in silence. With hands stuck deep in his denim pants pockets, Esteban kicked stones out of our path. I couldn't think of anything worth saying either.

Reaching school, we immediately heard Donald Riggsbee's loud, annoying voice: "I'd join up today if I was eighteen."

What a turnabout! Donald, the class braggart, had continually badgered me about the war. "Why should we bail out your stupid country again?" he had scoffed. "It's none of our business."

Pearl Harbor had clearly changed his mind. "Those monsters!" he exclaimed. "And guess what? They're rounding up Japs all over the West Coast. Gonna lock 'em up." He smirked. "Doesn't surprise me. I always thought the Japs were a tricky bunch."

"Is that so, Donald?" My eyebrows lifted scornfully. "Do you personally know any Japanese?"

"*Uh,* I think I met a Japanese gardener once," he muttered.

"Was he dangerous?"

"How can you be sure?" he retorted. "It's hard to tell one from the other."

"Rubbish!" I replied. "Before I came here, I thought all Americans were alike." I cast him a sly glance. "Now I know some Americans are quite clever and others are dumb."

"Oh yeah?" he sneered. "Well, the Japs just made a sneak attack on Pearl Harbor, killing thousands of Americans. And they may be planning to bomb all the cities on the West Coast. I'd say they're dangerous and devious."

He had me there. For I didn't know any Japanese people

11

either. Perhaps Donald was right, for once. Perhaps the Japanese were as awful as the beastly Nazis. As I fumbled for a reply, his pudgy face lit up. For once, he'd bested me!

On our walk home, Esteban sounded as rabidly patriotic as Donald. "I'd sign up for the U.S. Marines this minute if they'd let me."

"And break your mother's heart?" I asked quietly.

He shrugged. But later that afternoon, I heard her scolding him. "It's bad enough that all your cousins are gone, *'jito!*" she exclaimed. "We don't know where they are or if they're even alive! Now you want to disappear, too!" Usually Dolores was a gentle woman who never raised her voice. Hearing her stern words, I knew everything had changed. And I wondered—would anything be the same again?

CHAPTER THREE

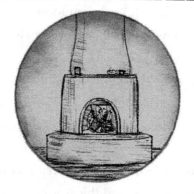

WAR. It was front page news every day. Family upon family was affected. On the Plaza, we cheered as a long line of young men signed up for combat. So many bright young faces, so many tearful mothers.

Life in our sweet adobe home, however, had remained much as usual. Every morning Clem grabbed her satchel and rushed off to the Indian Hospital. There, she battled against other fierce enemies: dysentery, tuberculosis and malnutrition.

I plugged away at school, giggled with Arabella, shyly glanced at Esteban and tried to ignore Donald's bluster.

Then came a shivery cold evening in January. The iron-gray skies promised snow. Soon the storm would hit the mountain peaks full blast. The streets would be blanketed with white. I didn't mind. Winter in Santa Fe had proved magical. I was always thrilled by the sight of snow-topped brown adobe walls and dazzling rows of icicles hanging from wooden *viga* ends.

This particular evening, Clem had settled into an armchair

after a long day at work. Burning piñon logs warmed the room giving off a sweet scent. I handed her a mug of tea from the kitchen. The prospect of snow had forced Dolores to go home early. She and Esteban and his four little sisters lived on top of Cerro Gordo, the "fat hill" adjacent to town. Trudging up that slope through snow wasn't easy. So she had left as soon as she'd finished her chores.

Clem was flipping through a stack of mail. I was curled up on the couch leafing through the *Saturday Evening Post*. A photo of a slender blonde in a scarlet cape caught my eye. *Would I ever look that gorgeous?*

"Fiddlesticks!" Clem declared, staring at a typed letter in her hand. "I shoulda' guessed this was coming."

"What?" I barely glanced up from the magazine.

"They want me," she responded.

I finally looked up. "Who wants you?"

"Uncle Sam."

"Your uncle?" I wondered why I hadn't heard of him before.

"Not exactly my uncle," Clem explained. "Uncle Sam is every American's uncle. He's like the King of England, except the king really exists and Uncle Sam doesn't."

A tiny frown wrinkled my brow. Was she teasing me? There was so much in America I still knew nothing about. Seeing me perplexed, Clem quickly explained, "He's a mythical character who represents our government."

"Oh yes, now I recall," I said. "The stern man on posters, dressed in red, white, and blue. He points his finger and commands every young man to register for the draft."

"That's him."

14

"So why's he writing you?" My stomach began to churn. "Does he want you to become a soldier?"

"Not a soldier. It's the nursing corps that wants me." Clem scanned the letter again.

"The nursing corps? They're like soldiers, aren't they?" My voice sounded shrill. "Last spring you plainly stated you'd never return to the battlefield. You said your job was *here*— caring for people in the pueblos and villages—old people, babies!" I pointed at the crackling flames. "Toss that letter in the fire where it belongs."

Clem took a moment before responding, "I did say that, Bea, and I meant it. But they're not asking me to return to the warfront." She paused. "They're asking me to train other nurses who are heading for war."

Her gaze was strong and level. I tried to return it but couldn't. After all, Clem was an excellent nurse. She'd be a superb teacher of nurses. Plus, she'd had plenty of experience. In 1917 she'd lied about her age in order to serve as a Red Cross nurse during the Great War. She knew blood and smoke and the heartache of sitting by a young man who wouldn't survive the night. The U.S. Army couldn't have selected a more qualified trainer.

"Where? Where would you go to train nurses?" I could hear the plaintive note in my voice.

"Washington, D.C.," she replied. "That's the center of the action these days."

I dropped my eyes and stared into the blazing logs in the fireplace. Inside I felt a muddle. I knew the real reason I didn't want her to go. I didn't want her to leave me—Beatrice Agatha Sims—the girl who had arrived on the train nearly a year and a half ago. The one wearing white cotton gloves and black patent-leather shoes. The spoiled, stuck-up girl who had never washed a dish or made her own bed.

Clem had steered me in another direction—not just to wash dishes and sweep the kitchen floor. Soon I had learned to clean out the chicken coop, change a truck tire, shovel snow and chase coyotes from the backyard. I very much liked the girl that I had become. And a large part of that was Clem's doing. What if she deserted me now?

I sank back on the sofa, silent for a moment. Then a grand idea struck and I leaned forward. "Washington," I exclaimed. "That's the capital of the United States, isn't it? I've heard it's a lovely city."

Visions of Clem and me living in Washington filled my head. Unlike dusty little Santa Fe, Washington was bound to be a real city with stores and theaters, buses and taxis and tearooms. A city like my beloved London!

Naturally I would miss Santa Fe and all my dear friends but, but...a smile broke through as I jumped up. "It will be an adventure. For the two of us."

Clem also smiled, though her eyes remained sober. "Bea, I'm afraid there can't be a *we* this time. It's gonna be a tough assignment—twelve to fifteen hour days, six or seven days a week. And there won't be a Dolores to back me up, like here."

Indignation fueled my reply. "You think I need you or Dolores looking after me?" I retorted. "I'm practically grown! I can fend for myself!"

Clem gazed at me fondly. "You have grown a lot. It's a pleasure to see. But thirteen is not adult. When your parents sent you here, they didn't intend for you to fend for yourself."

16

"Of course they didn't." I groped for a response. "But they'll understand. They know how important it is for all Americans to aid the war effort. And if that requires you going to Washington, then, then…" My arguments began to sound weak, even to me.

Clem simply shook her head. "Washington is flooded with people getting this country geared up for war. It's a huge operation. I don't know how I'll find a place for me. For two, it would be impossible."

She dropped the letter in her lap. "And, Bea…I've gotta go. I know too well what those young nurses are going to face. You can't really tell a person what it's like when twenty men on bloody litters are carried into a muddy tent…" She paused, biting her lip. "But I've got to get those gals ready as possible. So none of 'em feel as foolish and helpless as I did."

Of course Clem was right. There was no use in saying more.

And yet a lump had lodged in my throat. The very same lump that had stuck there when I had said goodbye to my family in England. It had never entirely disappeared. Soon Clem was going to disappear. Just as my family had vanished across the ocean. How unfair, how cruel!

My shoulders slumped, my arms hung limply at my sides. Clem came over and wrapped an arm around me. "We'll figure out something, kid. You're safe, you have friends, you're part of this community. And I won't be that far away, not a whole ocean away."

But I couldn't bear hearing another word. I pulled away from Clem and ran toward the stairs, wanting to escape to my room. "No indeed, not an entire ocean!" I shouted back. "But all the way across this country—this huge country. The United States is entirely too big, you know, entirely too big!"

I rushed up the stairs and flung myself on my bed, weeping. It didn't matter that I was thirteen and tall for my age. I was as upset as a five-year-old.

CHAPTER FOUR

Clem had only a few weeks to prepare for her trip to Washington. And, as usual, she didn't waste any time. Meanwhile I did my best to get over my upset. This was no time to childishly fuss and fume. What I needed was *gumption*—one of Clem's favorite words—meaning a spot of courage and a dab of boldness rolled into one. So far, I lacked much of either, but I aspired to more of both.

The war was forcing everyone, rich or poor, to behave differently. On the radio, we heard how President Franklin D. Roosevelt's wealthy sons had signed up for armed services. Meanwhile boys across the country were leaving cities and small towns, farms, ranches and Indian pueblos for the same purpose. If these young men could leave home and family to defend freedom, then surely I could adjust as well.

As Clem packed her things, she'd frequently glance at me thoughtfully. One evening as I hemmed a skirt, she said, "I've been thinking what to do with you, Bea."

"What to do with me?" I looked up, surprised.

"Where you're gonna live while I'm away."

My mouth fell open. "Why, I'm going to live right here."

She shook her head. "That's just the rub. Dolores isn't here all the time. Nights and weekends, she's with her family. Though we did talk about you moving up to her home on Cerro Gordo."

Live in her home? That tiny adobe on the hill? With four little girls and *Esteban*? The very idea warmed my cheeks. Imagine passing close by him as I went in and out of the bath, wrapped only in a towel. Actually, I wasn't sure their home even had an *indoor* bath.

"We both agreed it wouldn't work," said Clem, oblivious (I hoped) to my imaginings. "Not enough room."

Then she added, "Plus, Dolores is going to be far too busy. Many of her neighbors are losing sons to the army and navy—some are elderly or disabled. She'll have her hands full looking out for them." Clem looked thoughtful. "I gotta figure out some other place."

For me, the solution to the problem seemed obvious. I quickly declared, "Why don't I live with Arabella and Uncle Diego?" My best friend lived with her uncle because her mother, an opera singer, worked in large cities like New York and San Francisco. Arabella worshipped her mother and constantly praised her beauty, talent and generosity. Yet her mother rarely appeared in Santa Fe. In fact, I'd never once seen her.

Uncle Diego's house was very different from Clem's tidy bungalow. It was old and rambling with one room spilling into the next, and always in a jumble. Nor was there any sort of schedule for meals or bedtime or anything.

An artist, Uncle Diego often seemed to forget about meals altogether. Or he might prepare a giant pot of pinto beans that would last an entire week. Of course there was Lola, his fiancée and model, who hailed from Alabama. But she refused to go in the kitchen. "I had to cook suppa' for my po' family from the time I was six years ole 'til I left home at sixteen," she claimed. "And that's enuf cookin' for anybody."

So often when I visited, Arabella would scrounge up a meal from whatever she could find in the icebox or larder. She'd throw together all sorts of odd thing like noodles, canned mushrooms, tuna and tomato sauce. Then she'd create exotic names for her dishes, like Fiji Soup or Spaghettini Romanesca. Sometimes the meals were awful, but by then we were usually too hungry to care.

Clem shook her head. "I like Uncle Diego, but it seems like he's an awful puny sort of parent. Arabella practically has to raise herself, doesn't she?"

I responded with a slight shrug. Then I considered my best friend's disposition. Most of the time she was sunny and cheerful, but other times she plunged into a sadness she called "moping." Sometimes it took days for her to rally out of it.

"I'd prefer you lived with someone who can give you the sort of advice and support that I do," said Clem.

I stabbed the needle into the hem, barely missing my finger. Did she really think I couldn't cope on my own?

Clem continued, "There's someone I'd like you to meet who might be perfect." And that's how we were invited to dinner at the home of the wealthiest woman in Santa Fe, Elizabeth Amelia White.

21

When Arabella learned I was going to Miss White's home for dinner, her eyes bulged. "I've never been there. But I've heard it's a palace."

"Like Buckingham Palace?" I exclaimed.

"Are you kidding?" Arabella grimaced like I was a dim-wit. "It's a Spanish-Indian-Moorish palace. Like the Alhambra in Spain. Or the Taj Mahal in India. It's huge, with all sorts of terraces and a real swimming pool—the only one in Santa Fe. It's not like any place you've ever seen. Not like any place anybody's ever seen. Except maybe an Aztec princess." Arabella lowered her voice mysteriously. "She calls her home *El Delirio*."

"What does that mean?" I murmured.

"I have no idea," said Arabella. "But it sounds exotic, doesn't it?"

I had to agree. There were many fine English estates, but none called "El Delirio."

"And, I bet you get to pet those magnificent dogs," Arabella opined.

"Dogs?"

"Don't you remember? The other day? Near the Plaza?"

Then I did remember. The two of us had been heading downtown when we'd spied a small elegantly-dressed woman accompanied by several enormous dogs, long-haired and sil-very.

"Those dogs are gorgeous," I had murmured to Arabella.

She had nodded, beaming. "They're Irish wolfhounds."

Tears had sprung to my eyes. "*Irish* wolfhounds? My good-ness, they're as far from home as I am."

That had been a week ago. Now Arabella was gazing at

me eagerly. "Please, please let me go to dinner with you," she pleaded.

"I'll ask Clem," I replied, hoping she'd say yes. Somehow the prospect of El Delirio wasn't as appealing to me as it was to Arabella. Having a friend along might help.

CHAPTER FIVE

Days before I went to dinner at Miss White's, however, another noteworthy thing occurred. A new boy joined our class. I didn't notice him at first. Since he was male, however, Arabella had spotted him right off. "Look over there," she whispered, jerking her head in his direction. "I don't think he's very cute, do you?"

"Honestly, Arabella," I responded. "Do you have a cuteness yardstick you use to measure every boy you see?"

"Of course not," said Arabella, her lips curling in a little pout.

"I wonder why he's here," I mused. I could easily recall my first day at school in Santa Fe. How everyone stared. How my cheeks had burned. How I could barely mumble aloud my own name. Did he feel the same degree of shyness and embarrassment? Why had he arrived in the middle of the year? Had he relocated on account of the war? Lots of children were being forced to move from one place to another. Maybe he was one of them.

Glancing sideways, I attempted to examine him without his noticing. I needn't have bothered. He never looked up. He sat hunched over his desk as if guarding something precious. His straight, sandy hair fell in his face, partly concealing his pale, freckled skin. He was so narrow he looked as if he could glide through a crack in the door. I was reminded of the sort of dog you see in an alleyway, searching for something to eat behind the garbage bins.

Mrs. Lopez, our teacher, entered the room. Class would start in a few minutes. But I decided to approach the new boy anyway. Walking over to his desk, I said, "Good day, I was wondering if—"

That's as far as I got, because he jerked upright. "What… what do you want?" he growled, as if I'd kicked him in the shins.

"I…I was just wondering where you are from?" I stammered.

He frowned and I was almost certain he was going to say, "None of your business." Instead he said, "California." He stared at me a second or two. "Ever been there?" I shook my head.

"It's nice…and warm." He glanced out the window at the bare tree branches, shaken by a cold wind, then looked away.

I lingered another second, then returned to my desk. Arabella leaned over, hungry for information. I shook my head. I didn't know much, except that his gray eyes were a bit more appealing than his forbidding voice. And, yes, I felt almost certain he had been forced to come here. Most likely because of the war. That filled me with questions. Had he come with his family or on his own, like me? And if he was alone, where and with whom was he living?

I admit I was a bit nosy. But it also seemed like a good time for me to return favors. When I had first arrived, shocked and dismayed, Arabella had immediately rescued me. From the first day of school, she'd befriended me. Esteban had also soon become a pal. And Clem was always a support—kind and encouraging.

With this boy's rude manner, he wouldn't easily make friends. And if he didn't, he'd hate being here even more. Though it might be extremely difficult, I decided to become his friend. The moment I made that decision, the bell rang.

Mrs. Lopez smiled warmly. "Class, I hope you welcome our new student, Francis."

CHAPTER SIX

"No," Clem said firmly when I repeated Arabella's plea. "You're going to Miss White's to find out if you two get along. Then she may invite you to stay at her large house. So you need to make a good impression, with no distractions."

Ordinarily, Clem dressed very simply. At work as a nurse, she wore simple dresses. At home, she wore dungarees and boots. Her garb was practical—for in New Mexico one is perpetually battling wind, dust or mud. Fine clothes are rarely needed. In fact, the fancy frocks I'd brought from London remained in my trunk, rumpled and unused.

The evening we went to dinner at Miss White's, however, Clem insisted I wear a nice dress. She fussed over my hair for half an hour, though my dull-blond hair remained stubbornly straight. My looks hadn't been improved by growing taller; I was simply thinner and more gangly. My lovely mother must have feared that she'd hatched an ugly duckling. With Clem, however, looks were of little importance. "No one in my Oklahoma farm family was much of a 'looker'," she once told me. "But you couldn't meet a finer bunch, every one."

The night of the dinner party, however, Clem was clearly nervous. "Miss White always looks stylish," she murmured. "Like she's walking down Fifth Avenue in New York City."

Though I'd never visited New York, I knew just what she meant. Each month, I pored over the pages of *Harper's Bazaar* and *Vogue*. Some day I'd want to look stylish and I needed to figure out how.

For this important evening, we perused all the dresses that remained in the bottom of my trunk. Most were too short in the hem and a bit tight in the chest. Finally we found an outfit that suited: dark-blue serge with a round, white collar.

"Now you can help me get ready," announced Clem.

My eyes widened. "You?"

She nodded grimly. "I don't want to look like a hayseed from the sticks." Even though I was unfamiliar with these expressions, I knew just what she meant.

So I helped my chum pin up her sandy, gray-streaked hair in a neat bun, put on lipstick, a skirt, blouse, stockings. We even discovered a pair of heels in the bottom of the closet – not very high heels to be sure—but I hadn't known she even owned any.

As we walked to Miss White's house, she tottered a bit on the unfamiliar shoes and kept pressing back wisps of hair. "I'm just not used to high society," she mumbled.

I tried not to smile. How could a woman who could fix flat tires, brave snowy blizzards, and cope with a typhoid or diphtheria epidemic worry about a visit to a neighbor's house? Then I recalled the African explorer, Mary Kingsley. Father had slipped her biography into my trunk for inspiration. Miss

Kingsley, I learned, was one of the bravest women who've ever lived. She faced down poisonous snakes, lions and crocodiles. And yet she trembled at the thought of a London dinner party.

The distance between our house and Miss White's was only eight blocks. Yet it could have been on the other side of the world. That's how I felt when the door swung open.

"May I take your coat, miss?" asked the butler.

Nearly speechless, I handed him my coat with the barest nod.

Of course, I was very accustomed to butlers. There was one in our home in London and in Great-Aunt Augusta's and in nearly every home we visited. In fact, Great-Aunt Augusta's butler, Hadley, had chosen to remain in the city with her. He wished to make certain her standard of living didn't slip a notch.

But a butler in Santa Fe! I would have been far less surprised to see a cowboy in spurs or a mountain man draped in a bearskin. Yet, this butler had perfect manners, just as if he'd been whooshed here via a magic umbrella from London. He admitted us to the front foyer and announced our arrival to Miss White.

We entered a large, beautiful room. Like the sanctuary of a church, its high ceilings were crossed by dark beams. The windows were also high up and set deep in the thick walls. Plus, there was a long wooden balcony at one end that seemed ideal for a choir.

Miss White stood at the far end of the room. She was as small and delicate as her Irish wolfhounds were huge and powerful. Though she must have been at least 60, she held herself erect and her gaze was firm. Greeting me, her voice had a soft melodic quality. Yet I noticed her eyes were sad.

She introduced me to several other guests. Jack Lambert was a tall, handsome man, dressed like a cowboy in clean dungarees and boots. "Jack's in charge of our horses and many other things on the estate," said Miss White.

I smiled, wishing Arabella was at my side. She would have swooned—she loved cowboys!

"Hallo, lassie." A voice rang out from behind and I whirled around. A sturdy man with a kind face and twinkling blue eyes put out his hand. His other hand held a wooden pipe from which a plume of sweet smoke furled upward. "My name's Alex Scott. And I hear you and I are compatriots." A smile lit my face—how thrilling to hear a genuine Scottish brogue!

"Indeed, we are," I managed to murmur, taking hold of his large, calloused hand. Though Scotland and England had warred with one another in times past, the two had been joined as one nation for hundreds of years. I had often visited our neighbor to the North with my family and felt kin to its friendly, bold people.

I was so pleased to find a fellow Brit at the party, I could barely let loose of his hand. "Have you lived here long?" I asked quickly.

"Indeed, I have," he said smiling. "For quite some time. I tend to the hounds, you see."

With his pipe, he gestured toward the giant, long-haired dogs calmly sitting on the floor near the hearth. "You care for the Irish wolfhounds?" I asked.

Mr. Scott nodded proudly. "And no finer breed of dog exists anywhere in the world."

"May I stroke one?" I asked, eager to touch their long,

ash-colored coats.

"Of course you may, lassie. Nothing would make them happier."

Immediately I knelt down on the rug, and one of the dogs rested his huge, heavy head on my knees. "That's Gareth," said Mr. Scott. "He's a good 'un, he is."

Miss White piped up. "They're all good ones, aren't they, Alex?"

"They are, mum. Truly, every one of them is an excellent dog."

I remained on the floor for several minutes, petting Gareth and chatting with Mr. Scott. Meanwhile, Miss White spoke to Clem about health care on the pueblos. They both keenly wanted to improve health services.

Soon dinner was announced. We were seated at a very long dinner table, impeccably set with silver and china. For a moment, I panicked. Had I forgotten my table manners? No, of course not. In fact, when I glanced down at Clem, I could see she was observing me carefully as I chose which fork to use with which dish. My cheeks warmed with pleasure – for once, I could show Clem how to do something!

Our dinner was served by two servants, with the butler assisting. We dined on roast lamb with mint jelly, boiled potatoes with butter and parsley, and creamed spinach—the very sort of dinner I'd have in London. And there was île flottante for dessert, as light and frothy as a cloud. Though I'd grown to love the green chile and *frijoles* Dolores prepared for us every night, this was a special treat.

When it was time to leave, Alex invited me to return and view the kennels. "They're the finest kennels an Irish wolfhound ever slept in," he assured me. "And if you like to ride…"

I nodded eagerly.

"Then perhaps you'd like to accompany me sometime when I exercise the lot of them. It's a fine sight on a brisk winter's morn to see ten or twelve hounds running after the horses as we gallop across the fields."

My face shone with utter delight.

My head was fairly swimming with pleasant possibilities as we walked home. At the same time, something nagged at the corner of my mind. I wasn't certain of what until Clem spoke. "So you and Mr. Scott seemed to get on as quick as a scared jackrabbit?"

"Oh, we did," I quickly responded. "We did."

"And you didn't spend as much time with Miss White as I did, but I'm sure you got a fair impression of what sort of person she is."

"Oh yes, she seems like a fine lady."

"Well," said Clem. "That's settled then. She's a sharp, strong-minded woman. It will ease my mind for you to be there."

"I did notice that she seems a bit…" I started to say *sad*.

But Clem interrupted. "I bet you can move in next week, even before I'm gone. I'd like that."

I glanced over. Despite the shoes, her pace had quickened —she was so clearly happy to have found a good home for me in her absence. Yet, I started to drag my feet, as I slowly gathered my thoughts. In fact I was several feet behind when I finally spoke up. "It does seem ideal, but I'm not sure I *want* to live there."

"What?" She halted and turned to face me.

"Miss White's home is simply gorgeous, of course, and it's very tempting," I said. "But the more I think about it, the more certain I am—that's not where I want to live!"

"But why not, Bea?" Her face was worried.

"Honestly, Clem, think of all the new things I've learned in your home: fetching firewood, shoveling snow, raking leaves, feeding the chickens, weeding the garden." Reciting the list left me breathless. "I've learned so much I can hardly recall it all."

Clem nodded. "You're right. I'm proud of you."

"But don't you see what would happen if I go to live with Miss White?" My voice trembled. "In her grand household with the butler and servants and cook and yardmen—they'd do everything. Just like at my home in London. I'd have nothing to do. In a few weeks, I'd be as spoiled and useless as I used to be. I'd return to being the same girl as when I first arrived."

"I hope you're not implying that Miss White has nothing to do. She may be a very wealthy lady," said Clem, "but she works hard for the community."

I nodded. My mother was also very busy, at present. Before the war, she'd mostly planned dinner parties and shopped or went to tea with her friends. But now, like everyone else in England, she was pitching in to help. While in London, she had served up the bowls of soup that Cook had prepared for the homeless. Now in Dorset, she assisted at a hospital. Though admitting she'd faint at the sight of blood, Mother worked in the office, ordering supplies. "It's practically like planning a dinner party," she had written to me. "Only instead of twelve couples, we're now feeding one hundred fifty wounded men."

Still, imagining my life at Miss White's palace, I feared a

relapse to my old self. That spoiled, helpless girl that every-one—especially Esteban—had scoffed at. "Please, Clem, please understand."

Clem remained silent all the way back to the house. Finally, as she opened the door, she turned to me. "I'm glad you enjoy being helpful. Once you've got a taste for that, it's hard to be any other way."

I must have looked doubtful, for she added, "We'll see where else you could live." She sighed. "Though there's not much time."

CHAPTER SEVEN

For another few days, I continued to observe the new boy at school. He was doing everything possible to remain friendless. He barely spoke or looked at anyone in the eye, He refused to join in any games or sports. Francis seemed to live behind a high fence with a "No Trespassing" sign out front.

Still, I had made the decision to befriend him. So at lunchtime one day, I left the table where I was sitting with Arabella and marched up to him. He was peering around the room, searching for the most remote table. Before he reached that lonely outpost, however, I rushed over. "Hallo. Your name is Francis, isn't it? What a lovely name."

"Is not." He frowned. "It's a sissy name!"

"It isn't a sissy name!" I declared. "I have a cousin named Francis who's a captain in the RAF this very minute. That's the Royal Air Force, in case you don't know. And what about Captain Francis Drake, the explorer? Why, he was nearly as bold as the African explorer Mary Kingsley."

His frown deepened. "I've heard of Francis Drake, but who's Mary what's-her-name?" His face softened a bit, however, as if part of him was fighting to hold out against me while another part wanted to be friends. "And how come you know so much about explorers?"

"Books. I love to read," I said. "And I have an excellent biography of Mary Kingsley. In case you'd like to borrow it." Then I added something Clem had told me. "It's not surprising you don't know about Mary. Most history books don't tell anything about women explorers."

"I didn't know that," he said cautiously. "Maybe I will borrow it."

Seeing his expression begin to open up, I quickly exclaimed, "That's terrific—we're both interested in explorers. When shall we talk more?" His face immediately began to tighten, so I eagerly added, "About explorers and things."

With a suspicious tone he muttered, "I don't have much time."

I persisted. "At the Plaza after school? You've been there, haven't you?"

His frown returned. "I do chores after school."

"Yes, of course." I began to think that despite my strenuous efforts, I might not succeed in making a friend of Francis. Yet I was determined to give it another shot. "How about now?" I suggested, indicating the lunchroom. "We could sit together and talk."

He glanced toward the table where Arabella and others were sitting. "Don't you wanna sit with your friends?"

I shrugged. "Why don't you join us? There's room."

His gaze focused on the table for an instant. Five boys and

girls were casually smiling, talking and joking. A few were amiably trading carrots for apples or bologna for peanut butter sandwiches. Francis's face revealed a tiny, bright window of yearning before shutting down hard. "Nah, not today. Don't feel like it."

He turned and walked away. His shoulders were tightly hunched. I saw he gripped a 4 cent milk carton and a slim, very wrinkled brown paper bag. I wondered what was inside the bag—not much, I figured. And maybe it was nothing he wanted others to see.

Esteban had once told me that on his first day of third grade, his mother had packed a burrito for him—a rolled-up tortilla with beans and cheese inside. When he got it out for lunch, several boys sneered. "That all you got, *baboso*? Your ma ain't got any store-bought bread?"

He said he threw out the burrito that day and went hungry for lunch. The next day, he asked his uncle Nogales for a shoeshine kit and started shining shoes on the Plaza. With the first few dimes he earned, he went to the store, bought a loaf of white bread, and gave it to his mother. "Make real sandwiches from now on," he commanded her.

I rejoined Arabella at the table. "What in the world were you doing?" She gazed at me, astonished. "He's the sorriest-looking kid that ever walked in the door."

"I know," I replied.

"Like those dogs that whimper when anyone comes near."

"I know."

She looked at me earnestly. "Who do you think you are? Clara Barton?"

"Who's Clara Barton?

"You don't know who Clara Barton was? She was the first woman nurse."

"She was *not* the first woman nurse," I snapped. "Florence Nightingale was the first female nurse. Everyone knows that."

"Oh yeah, now I remember. Clara was the first *American* female nurse. She nursed soldiers on the Civil War battlefield."

"Well, she probably learned how from Florence," I responded.

"Probably." Arabella promptly changed the subject—her grasp of history was always shaky—and turned to her favorite topic. "What do you have for lunch? Anything interesting?" She'd already cleaned her plate of the meat and vegetables served in the cafeteria.

"Not really." I showed her what Dolores had packed.

"Oh no! A liverwurst sandwich?" She wrinkled her nose, then peered around the table in case anyone else had something to offer. No one did. She sighed and turned back to me. "What did you talk about?"

"Explorers," I mumbled, my mouth half full of bread and liverwurst.

"Explorers? What a funny thing to talk about. You must be desperate."

"I am desperate. He's a hard one to figure out."

"Why bother? He's not even a little…" She paused, trying desperately to imagine a word besides *cute*. "He's not very attractive," she finally spit out.

"Not in the conventional sense, it's true." I shrugged. "But I believe there's something there."

"Well, you could say that about everyone, I guess," Arabella responded, glancing around the lunchroom.

40

Just then, the ninth-grade class entered the cafeteria. Among these students was a stocky boy with thick, curly black hair named Henry Jenkins. His friends called him "Hank." He had loads of friends always clustered around. Arabella was so smitten with Hank that a tremor passed through her, just seeing him. Her eyes immediately locked on him and she could barely utter a word. Quite unusual for Arabella.

I'm afraid I found it rather amusing.

"Well, there he is, your Romeo," I murmured, nodding toward Hank. "You can float through the rest of the afternoon. You'll only miss geometry, geography, and P.E."

"Who cares?" Arabella murmured, her attention still glued in his direction.

An instant later, however, a large, statuesque, red-haired woman appeared, filling the cafeteria doorway. "My goodness, whose mother is she?" I murmured to myself.

The redhead was wearing a full-length fur coat and a dashing forest-green hat with a white feather. She would have stood out in any crowd, but among eighth graders in the Harrington Junior High cafeteria, she drew all eyes. Only Arabella, whose gaze was still fixed on Hank, had missed seeing her. The statuesque woman, however, definitely spied Arabella—whose own red curls always stood out. A resounding voice rang out. "My sweet, my darling angel, there you are at last!"

Then the large, buxom woman rushed toward us and swooped down on Arabella. The two immediately engaged in a tremendous hug while all the students stared, mouths hanging open. It was so operatic, I was tempted to applaud. That would have been appropriate, of course, for the woman was Arabella's mother, home at last.

Watching as tears of joy ran down Arabella's pink cheeks, I felt like crying, too. How glad she was! How she had longed for this moment! How I wished my own mother would appear in the cafeteria in exactly the same way!

Now I understood why Arabella and I had become such fast friends. Neither of us had a mother close at hand. We had to depend on letters or, in her case, infrequent long-distance calls. Now her mother was present but mine was still distant. Moreover, in a very short while I wouldn't even have Clem or her cozy home. Suddenly I felt more bereft than I had since landing on this strange continent.

Hadn't I been foolish to turn down the opportunity of staying at El Delirio? It was, at least, a warm, safe, solid lodging – which was more than many possessed in these turbulent times. And if I didn't stay there, then where? Was it entirely Clem's responsibility to find me a place or should I be pitching in to help?

As I glanced back at the joyous twosome, chattering away next to me, an idea began hatching in my brain.

CHAPTER EIGHT

As soon as Arabella composed herself, she introduced me to her mother. She didn't call her "Mother," however; she introduced her as Ariadne Starke and called her Ariadne. Once Arabella had confided to me that this was actually her mother's stage name. "Her real name is Ermine Gulag," explained Arabella. "But how could an opera singer be named Ermine Gulag?"

When the two finally drew apart, Arabella gestured to me. "Here's my very best friend, Beatrice." Ariadne immediately put her hand over her heart. "I've heard a lot about you, Beatrice. And naturally any friend of Arabella's is very dear to me." Then she grabbed hold and pressed me to her large bosom.

As soon as she released me, I turned to Arabella and said quite sincerely, "I've been very fortunate to know Arabella – no one could have a truer, kinder friend." Speechless, Arabella reached for my hand.

"I would have felt much further from home and family if Arabella hadn't interceded." I murmured, adding, "Both Arabella and Clem have been absolutely instrumental to my happiness. Though now with Clem leaving for Washington…"

I planned to add, "…I'll need a new home." But as I observed the two, it didn't appear as if any ray of awareness would penetrate the fog of their happiness. It might have been an even tearier moment except that Ariadne's current beau, Stanley, suddenly stepped forward. No one had previously noticed Stanley. That's because he was standing behind Ariadne. He was short, while she was tall; his voice was soft and low, while hers was loud and bold; he was as undramatic as she was dramatic. Yet he clearly adored Ariadne and she seemed equally enamored of him.

In fact, I was rather reminded of Uncle Diego and his passion for Lola when I saw Ariadne and Stanley cooing over each other. When I was with Clem later, I mentioned that fact and she said, "Ariadne and Diego are brother and sister so perhaps romance runs in their blood."

In fact my friend and her mother finally grasped the needs of someone outside themselves. The next day the two appeared at our door with Stanley close behind. I greeted them, hoping I didn't look overly expectant.

"We'd like to speak with Miss Pope," declared Ariadne as I ushered the small group inside.

Clem came out of the kitchen, wiping her hands on a dishtowel. She was eager to meet Arabella's mother, after all she'd heard. When everyone was introduced, Clem invited the guests to sit down. "If you can find a place." The normally tidy room was in disarray, with packing boxes in every corner.

"Actually, that's the reason for our visit," said Ariadne. "We know you plan to leave very soon for Washington."

Clem nodded. "On Tuesday."

Ariadne glanced at Stanley and then winked at me. "We just want you to know we'd love for Beatrice to stay with us."

Arabella could barely conceal her glee. Turning with excitement to Clem, she squealed, "Can she? Can she? You will let her, won't you?" I too turned toward Clem, trying to conceal my excitement behind a poker face.

Clem was quiet a moment. "I appreciate your offer, Ariadne, and I know you mean well. But do you know how long you'll be staying in Santa Fe?"

Ariadne fell silent; it was clear she hadn't considered that topic at all, however, Stanley firmly stepped forward. He spoke in a quiet, steady voice. "It's hard to know anything these days. As you well know, the country's in an uproar." He glanced fondly at Ariadne. "That's why I think it's smart to stay someplace like Santa Fe. A little town in the middle of nowhere. Who's gonna bomb us here?"

Then he explained how German submarines had been spotted off the eastern coast of the United States. "So you see, even Long Island, where I come from, isn't safe. As for the west coast, people in California and Oregon and Washington state are terrified of a Japanese attack. If Jap bombers could surprise folks at Pearl Harbor, they could do the same in San Diego or Seattle. People are jittery. That's why they're pulling up all the Japanese who live in those parts and sending them inland. They're being put in camps all over the West."

Clem didn't seem surprised. "I've heard and it's really very sad how people—some who have lived here all their lives—

45

are being uprooted from their homes." She sighed, adding, "There's a rumor some are coming here."

I was shocked. "Coming to Santa Fe?"

Stanley shrugged. "They wanna put the Japanese somewhere far from the coast, so why not here?"

"But that…that would be awful, wouldn't it?" Ariadne murmured, turning to Stanley.

He put a reassuring arm around her. "I don't think so. I've dealt with lots of Japanese-American shopkeepers in my grocery business. And they were always quite trustworthy." He added, "Not a bit like those German Nazis. And whatever people say, the ones here got nothing to do with the Kamikazi pilots flying straight from Japan."

Everyone was silent a second, no doubt contemplating how many crazy things were happening at once.

"So it seems you do plan to stay here a while?" said Clem, reminding us of the original reason for the visit.

Ariadne beamed. "Oh yes, I had forgotten how much I love Santa Fe—the mountains, the clean air, the friendly people. And, of course, I just adore being with my darling girl." She gave her daughter a big squeeze.

Arabella's face was joyful. She grabbed her mother's hand and mine too, holding both tightly. Only Clem remained quiet and thoughtful, finally gazing at me. "What do you think, Bea? Want some time for us to talk about it?"

I knew Clem was giving me a chance to say no in a graceful manner. She clearly still had some doubts about the arrangement. And, truthfully, I had a few myself but I had conveniently tucked them far away. "It's the best plan possible," I declared boldly. "There couldn't be a better place for me to live in all Santa Fe."

Clem eyed me another second and then said, "Okey-dokey. Beatrice can move over to your house." She cautiously added, "If things change…well, she'll let me know."

Forgetting we should behave like grownup young ladies, Arabella and I jumped up and down, giggling. Stanley kissed Ariadne's cheek. Ariadne declared she and Stanley would love to fix Clem a big farewell dinner. "You can invite all your friends to say goodbye and wish you well."

Clem thanked her. "I'm afraid I won't have time. I want to go by as many neighboring villages and pueblos as possible." Just mentioning these, her eyes filled with tears. She quickly excused herself, saying she needed to finish cleaning up.

All of a sudden, I realized why she had looked troubled during the last few weeks. It wasn't simply her concern for me. What about the people in remote Hispanic villages and Indian pueblos? All the people she had cared for during the past fifteen years? Before the war, there had been little enough in supplies or medicine or nurses or doctors for them. What would there be now?

Her concerns, I admit, quickly left my mind. I was too pleased about the possibility of sharing a room with Arabella. On the few occasions we had overnighted, we'd talked on and on and on until reluctantly falling asleep. We had shared views on school, our families, our friends, books, movies, food—just about everything. My only concern was Arabella's current obsession with Hank. I was afraid I might perish of boredom if she talked endlessly about him. But I put that worry out of my mind as I said goodbye to Ariadne, Stanley and Arabella, knowing I'd soon see plenty of them.

Alone again while Clem busied herself in the kitchen, I began to wonder if there was anyone I could talk about with Arabella with the fervor she discussed Hank. Esteban remained my very particular friend. The one who caused my heart to jump whenever he walked in the door. The one who could tease me endlessly and I'd forgive because he was so (yes, that was the word) *cute*. Yet often I felt shy when his name came up. Usually I denied to Arabella and even to myself that I had any special feelings about him. I certainly couldn't chatter on and on, as Arabella did about Hank.

Then, of course, there was Francis, the new kid. He was certainly not a romantic interest, yet he still intrigued me. And I still had many questions about him.

To my surprise, the answers arrived sooner than expected.

CHAPTER NINE

Since Clem was leaving on Tuesday, I begged to stay home from school on Monday. She was departing on the *Silver Chief* train for Washington, D.C. from the train station in Lamy, about 20 miles south of town, where I had arrived the previous year. Since she was boarding at 5:30 a.m., however, I wouldn't accompany her to the station.

She reluctantly agreed to let me stay out of school for our final day together. It turned out to be a gloomy day indeed. Everything in the house was packed in boxes and crates and neatly labeled. All the furniture had been carefully covered with sheets. The rugs had been rolled up. Dolores had scrubbed the shelves in the kitchen, so no trace of food would invite an invasion of mice. The foodstuffs had been given away. The chickens had been transported to the house on Cerro Gordo where Esteban could tend them.

I had carried a large carton of flour, sugar, salt, and other staples to Arabella's house. Her mother was extremely grateful. "I expect we'll be baking lots of cakes and pies and muffins together," she announced, beaming at Arabella, who stood at her side. I had noticed my friend rarely let her mother out of her sight, as if the woman might vanish if she did.

Clem and I sat glumly amid the boxes as she checked and rechecked her list. I tried to divert myself—sewing on buttons, playing a game of solitaire, reading the morning news, top to bottom—but nothing held my interest. And I was far more uneasy about Clem's departure than I wished anyone to know. How would I ever manage without her warm encouragement? That familiar lump from the past lodged again in my throat.

She must have noticed. "Let's go down and get an ice-cream soda at Zook's," Clem suggested.

It seemed a perfect distraction. "I'll grab my coat," I exclaimed, running to fetch it.

Arm in arm, we walked down to the Plaza. The streets were nearly deserted as a harsh February wind tossed the few remaining leaves every which way. The Plaza was also nearly empty. A few shoppers, bundled in heavy coats and scarves, hurried in and out of the shops along the perimeter of this large public square.

At the Zook's Pharmacy counter, a pig-tailed girl took our orders. Her eyebrows shot up. "Ice-cream sodas? Today?"

As she was scooping out the ice cream, I glanced around. No one else was buying ice cream or sodas. There was a short queue of people at the pharmacy window.

Then I gasped with surpise. My schoolmate, Francis, was sitting on the floor next to the newspaper and magazine racks. He was more hunched than usual, intently reading something. I excused myself and left Clem at the counter.

Francis didn't notice me approach. "Hallo," I said. "Funny to see you here." He looked up, frightened, like a rabbit spotted by a fox. "Wh- what are you doing here?"

Nodding toward Clem, I started to explain who she was and why she was leaving. Somehow, my entire history tumbled out—from leaving bombed-out London to arriving in sunny Santa Fe and nearly everything that had happened since. Finally I paused for air, wondering why I had entrusted a near-stranger like Francis with my personal saga.

He nodded, however, as if he understood, then glanced around guiltily. "So are you gonna tell?"

"What? That you're dodging school?"

He nodded.

I shrugged. "No reason for that. Though I am curious…"

"What?"

"What you're reading? You seem to love it!" I tried to eye the cover. Without replying, he thrust out a comic book.

"*Captain America*," I read aloud. "So what do you think?"

He grinned and poked the tall stack. "These came this morning. That's why I couldn't wait 'til school let out. Might all be gone by then."

I peered at the slim, colorful magazine in his hands. "Good reading, huh?"

"It's not the writing, it's the pictures I like," he responded, adding shyly. "I draw pictures myself, you see."

I observed Francis more keenly. Was he a budding artist? Perhaps I should introduce him to Uncle Diego.

"Why read them here?" I asked. "You could purchase one and read at home. Or at school." I often hid novels behind my textbooks and read while I was supposed to be studying.

"Why *not* read 'em here?" His lower lip swelled out belligerantly. "Why waste a quarter?"

Oh dear. Sometimes I did forget everyone didn't enjoy the posh life my family had afforded me. Francis probably didn't possess an extra quarter. To save him any further embarrassement, I quickly changed the subject. "Please come meet my friend Clem. And you could have some ice cream too?" Francis started to shake his head and it occurred to me that if he hadn't a quarter for his most favorite comic book, he certainly didn't have one for ice cream. So I quickly lied, "I happen to have quite a lot of extra change with me today—birthday money. Far more than I need, so another cone or two would make no difference whatsoever. What flavor do you like?"

His eyes narrowed as if he couldn't believe I was serious. So I continued speaking rapidly. "Some people don't care to eat ice cream when it's freezing cold outside. But I just think it makes it more special." By now he'd stood up and was eyeing the ice cream advertisements behind the counter. Encouraged, I continued. "And since Clem's leaving tomorrow, this will be your only chance to meet her."

Either my words or the enticement of ice cream seemed to convince him and we headed over. If Clem was surprised to see Francis, she didn't show it. She had an awfully good poker face.

"Let me introduce a fellow student, new to the class, Francis *uh* …"

"McKetchum," he said, hesitantly putting out his hand to Clem.

She seized it in her firm grasp. "Pleased to meet you, Francis."

"Francis likes to draw. In fact, I interrupted him as he was studying the pictures in the latest *Captain America*." I imagined that by using the word "study" I could justify his not being in school.

"A lot of artists come to Santa Fe," said Clem, eyeing him warmly. "But I guess you knew that."

"Artists? Here?" Francis looked startled. He obviously had no idea.

"So why did you come to Santa Fe?" I had been desperate to ask from the moment I first saw him. Now was my opportunity.

The question, however, clearly made him uncomfortable. He shuffled his feet before answering, "I came to live with my uncle. Kevin McKetchum. Know him? He works at the State Penitentiary."

"Don't think I've met Mr. McKetchum," Clem responded. "But lots of people in town work there. Is he a guard?"

"Yep." Francis nodded, a bit uneasy.

"You left California to come live with him?" I asked, observing him carefully. Clem flashed me a warning look. I knew it wasn't polite to be so nosy. But Francis didn't seem to mind.

"My mom and me lived in San Diego. 'Til she got a factory job and wasn't hardly home. And Dad—he's been on a Navy troop carrier for two years. From even before the war."

He bit his lip. "I didn't want to come. Not at all. Have you ever seen San Diego? It's warm there and pretty. With lots of plants and flowers everywhere."

He so clearly missed his former home, I regretted even asking him about it. To repent, I quickly asked, "What flavor ice cream do you prefer? They have chocolate, vanilla, strawberry, and orange sherbert."

His face brightened. "Chocolate. A chocolate cone, if that's okay."

"Absolutely." I signaled for the teenaged girl behind the counter. "One chocolate cone, double scoop."

We chatted a bit about school and explorers. I didn't dare bring up the subject of his family or reasons for coming. As soon as he finished his cone, Francis muttered thanks. Then he reluctantly dropped the comic book back on the stack and slipped out of the pharmacy. I wasn't certain I'd made any progress in our friendship. He certainly was an odd duck.

CHAPTER TEN

The sky had begun to lighten as Clem and I walked back home together, arm in arm. It wasn't nearly as cold. The sun had slipped out from behind the clouds and the bright orb was now warming the afternoon air. A newsboy had ventured out and stood on a corner selling the latest edition. Clem paused to purchase one.

A tall, very thin, blond man stood nearby. He'd just bought a newspaper and was studying the front page. Glancing up, he doffed his hat and said, "Good afternoon." His look was a trifle sharp. And even in those few words, I could hear a distinct foreign accent.

For a second I wondered where he was from. Santa Fe often lures foreign visitors. Many more, however, in the summer months than now. And somehow this man didn't resemble a tourist.

As we walked on, Clem interrupted my wondering. "I'm glad to see you're reaching out to that boy in your class," she said. "It's hard to feel sorry for yourself when you're helping someone else."

"Oh, Clem," I squeezed her arm. Somehow she always seemed to guess my feelings. "Honestly, it's hard to imagine carrying on without you."

She tightened her grip on my hand. "Honestly, Bea, I believe you'll do fine. You've got more gumption than you think. Remember that! And probably more common sense than most folks in Arabella's house. If there's any trouble at all, don't waste time. Contact me or somebody you trust." She paused and gazed directly at me. "Okay, Bea? Promise? Don't let things go too far before turning them around."

I nodded, hoping to seem confident. Inside, however, I was fervently praying things *would* go well. And that I wouldn't require any "gumption." Or need to call on anyone for help.

Reaching home, I checked the post and was pleased to find a letter from Mother. Her letters were always a pleasant distraction, rarely containing more than a few shreds of information about the war.

Dear Beatrice,

I hope this finds you well. I'm thrilled to bring you good news. You have a new baby cousin. Elizabeth had her fourth child early Saturday morning. A beautiful baby girl—bald as an old man—but with long, dark lashes. The names under consideration are Evelyn, Eloise or Elinor. Do you have a preference? If you write immediately, your selection might be considered. Whatever her name is, the child will join her two brothers and her sister in the nursery upstairs.

We've got quite a household of women here—with men only popping in for weekends when they get time off. That goes for the servants, as well.

The butler, the chauffeur, and the gardener are all off serving our country in one capacity or another. So we're like you—eagerly awaiting the post each day to find out how they're faring. So far the news has all been good. That leaves Elizabeth's oldest son, Freddy, as the "man of the house" at age 8. I believe he really relishes that position and may be upset when any other males return. Give my best to Miss Pope. We received her letter and know she plans to leave for Washington soon. We're so grateful for all the American help being poured into the war effort. And we know she will leave you in a solid and safe situation.
Much love,
Mother

As usual, I read the letter several times over. I relished the news, of course, but also the scrawl of her handwriting and the scent of the paper like lavender soap. It all reminded me intensely of Mother and of home.

Putting aside the letter, I wondered briefly about Francis. Was he receiving any letters from his mother? Since she worked long hours in a factory, she might not have the time to write. What about his father? I'd heard that men on ocean vessels often had long hours to fill. I hoped he did write and often. Letters would do a lot to cheer up Francis.

Well, I firmly told myself, don't ask. It's his business, not yours.

My reverie was interrupted by Clem pointing to an article. "Look at this headline: *Dogs for Defense*." Reading further, she explained, "The U.S. military needs dogs. So they're asking people across the country to offer their pets."

"Their pets?" I was shocked. "Does that mean little pooches like my sweet Alfie back in London might go war?"

"Not every dog will be chosen. They're looking for dogs that are fifty pounds or more—big dogs like German Shepherds or collies or Doberman Pinschers," said Clem. She put down the newspaper, recalling another time. "I saw dogs working during World War I. The French and Belgian soldiers had quite a few."

"But what do dogs do in battle?"

"Oh my gosh, they use their sharp noses and ears. They can be trained to smell out hidden bombs," said Clem. "At night they serve as sentries, guarding the soldiers. They carry messages from one post to another—traveling across dangerous territory. They save lives."

"Big dogs?" My mind started turning. The biggest dogs in town belonged to Miss White. "I bet Irish wolfhounds would make great military dogs. Do you think Miss White would offer hers to the army?"

"I don't know," Clem answered. "They're trained for dog shows, not combat."

"I will speak to her and Mr. Scott." What an exciting idea. "Perhaps they'll let me help too."

Clem gazed at me fondly. "I knew you'd figure out a way to be helpful. And it would keep you in contact with Miss White."

"You still wish I were staying with her, don't you?" I said.

"I do a little," Clem admitted. "Ariadne is extremely nice and has the best of intentions. However, it's been quite a while since she's lived in a little town like Santa Fe. Or been a mom. She's used to playing lots of different roles but not that one. As for Mr. Tesch, he seems like a steady sort of fellow, but I barely know him. And sometimes Ariadne hasn't shown such great judgment about men." She smiled at me. "Like I said, you have more good sense than the lot of them, so use it!"

I gazed back at her, a tiny frown wrinkling my brow. Indeed, I too had some questions. I wondered about the disorder of Arabella's home—the lack of proper times for meals or bedtime or study or cleanup or anything. Would that change now that Ariadne and Stanley were in charge? Or might the chaos grow even worse? As for meals, all I'd heard about so far were cakes and pies and muffins—would they eat any solid food beforehand?

I'd find out quickly, once I moved in. And that would be very soon.

CHAPTER ELEVEN

It was still completely dark when the alarm rang at 5:00 a.m. next morning. I jumped up to say goodbye to Clem and give her one long last hug. Then she departed, and I hurried back to my room and jumped under the warm covers.

I didn't go back to sleep, however. Too many things to consider. The house already seemed quite empty, and Clem had only been gone a few minutes. Finally I heard the backdoor slam and knew Dolores had arrived. She'd put wood in the cookstove in the kitchen. Once it warmed up, she'd start fixing breakfast.

I lay in the warm bed, thinking how I'd grown used to breakfast in this house. Dolores bustling around the woodstove, Esteban seated nearby at the kitchen table. He pretended to ignore me until he could come up with something humorous or annoying. Leaping out of bed, I trembled with more than the morning chill—today would be our last breakfast together, perhaps for a very long while. I rushed toward the kitchen, not wishing to miss a precious moment.

They must have had the same concern. Dolores turned to me with a big smile as soon as I entered the kitchen, "Hope you're hungry, *'jita*. I've fixed a special breakfast *muy grande*." She invited me to sit at the table. There she spooned out two fried eggs, refried pinto beans, fried *papitas*, several slices of crisp bacon (tasty American, not English bacon), warm tortillas, plus toast. Beside my plate was a jar of apricot jam that Dolores had made from the apricot tree in the backyard. To me, it was the best jam in the world because I had picked the ripe juicy fruit myself. Then I'd watched as Dolores ladled the thick sweet jam into glass jars. She had already promised I could take a few with me to Arabella's.

As I was spreading some onto my toast, Esteban appeared. His mother quickly prepared a plate for him as well. Unlike Dolores, however, he wasn't smiling. In fact, he barely glanced in my direction. Instead he studied the two eggs on his plate as if they might leap off if not carefully observed. Why was he in such a foul mood? He wasn't the one forced to leave this cozy little house.

Twenty minutes later, Esteban and I headed toward school as usual. An icy wind whipped our cheeks though the sky was a pale blue, without a cloud in sight. Esteban kept his head low, his eyes directed toward the sidewalk ahead. After a short distance, I finally broke the silence. "Is everything all right?"

He didn't reply so I added, "Any news of your cousins?"

He shook his head, then kicked a stone on the pavement out of the way. "Not much. We just know it's tough over there right now, really ugly." He glanced over quickly. I nodded. He fell silent again. After a long, quiet moment, I hazarded another question. "Is…is something wrong?"

Esteban hesitated, struggling for words. Finally he spoke, still not looking at me. "It's just…I wonder…I wonder if you'll still talk to me when we're not…I mean you're not, not…when you don't have to."

I felt my eyebrows shoot up. "*Don't have to speak to you?*" I stopped dead in the middle of the sidewalk. "Do you imagine I speak to you because I *must?*"

"Well, I don't know," he muttered. "I guess I don't know…" He finally paused, gazing earnestly at me. "I mean, will you? When we don't eat breakfast together? And we don't walk to school together and, and…stuff?"

By now we were standing across the street from the school. I knew we couldn't remain here long, talking. Just seeing us together, Esteban's friends would tease him unmercifully.

So I hastened to respond, "Of course I shall, Esteban. Of course! Because…because I like you." Without thinking, I reached out and touched his hand.

First, he glanced down at the touch my fingers, as if it truly meant something. Then with the hint of a smile, he replied, "Yeah, well, okay." Then he turned and began racing across the street toward his buddies. So I may have only imagined hearing him toss out the words, "I like you, too."

I watched him join his friends in the schoolyard, then I walked slowly across the street. My heart was beating much stronger than usual and it needed to quiet down before I headed for school. I had taken for granted that Esteban and I would continue as friends even with my change in address. Yet he was right, it wouldn't be so easy to be together. We'd have to make a point of it. And seeing us together, purposefully, might cause other students to snicker or make fun of us. And that prig Donald Riggsbee would surely jest about it. He always looked for some way to make me uncomfortable.

Though I might be able to ignore this foolishness, I doubted Esteban could. He hated to be teased by his buddies.

Suddenly my heart felt as heavy as a water-soaked mattress. First Clem had departed. Then I'd had my final breakfast in the warm, cozy kitchen with Dolores. Now it appeared that Esteban and I might cease to enjoy the jovial, silly, sympathetic fun we had always had together. These three were the people I most counted on each day, aside from Arabella. And my dear girlfriend was so distracted these days by her mother, she was hardly able to give me much attention. I looked down at my two shoes—sturdy British Oxfords—now they would need to carry me, me alone, into a future I couldn't anticipate.

CHAPTER TWELVE

Upon reaching my desk that morning, I discovered a book on top called *Great Explorers of the World*. Francis stood nearby observing me closely. "What do you think? Do you like it? I found it in the library."

I thumbed through the pages. "Christopher Columbus, Marco Polo, Henry Hudson, Ferdinand Magellan, Francis Drake, Lawrence of Arabia." I looked up. "What do they all have in common?"

He looked puzzled.

"All men, just like Clem said." I sighed. "According to most history books, no woman has ever left her backyard."

"You don't want to read it?" He reached for the book.

"Oh, I do." I replied, holding it close. "It's just...I don't know. It's a little disappointing."

His thin face softened. "I know what you mean."

"You do?" I was surprised.

"A lot of things aren't fair." He hastily turned and started back to his seat.

"Thank you," I called after him, holding up the book. "Thanks for thinking of me."

I suppose I had expected a smile or a nod or some sort of reaction. But Francis had returned to his desk, with his back to me, as if we'd never spoken. I shook my head—I had taken on a bit of a challenge.

Arabella arrived at school an hour late. She'd been fixing up *our* room, she said, winking at me. Well, that was a nice surprise—at least I was welcome somewhere.

Indeed, when we arrived there after school, Arabella had clearly gone to some trouble. The pile of clothes, papers, books, and candy wrappers that normally littered the floor were almost gone. (Though I later discovered them in a heap on the closet floor.) She had pushed aside her dresses to give mine space in the closet. And she'd emptied two drawers for my sweaters, socks, nightgowns, and undies. Plus, there was a marvelous smell coming from the kitchen.

"Ariadne and Stanley are planning a stupendous dinner," said Arabella with a radiant smile. "Stanley is an amazing chef. Every night we feast on food from a different country—Greece, China, Italy, Russia."

"My goodness! Has he been to all those places?"

"Oh no, he's only lived in New York City. But people from all those countries live in New York," she explained. "And he was in the grocery business, so he was often invited to their homes for a meal."

Indeed, dinner was wonderful, a thick French soup filled with all sorts of seafood called *bouillebaise*. I couldn't help wondering how the clams and eels had made the journey to

Santa Fe—a town far from any seashore. Stanley, I guessed, had many special connections.

The six of us were squeezed around the table—Ariadne and Stanley, Arabella and me, and Uncle Diego and Lola. Afterward we were treated to an aria by Ariadne. I was staggered; she had such an amazing voice. Though wearing only a simple housedress and a scarf on her head, she transformed the room into a splendid opera hall.

Glancing over, however, I saw that Lola's eyes had narrowed. A voluptuous, raven-haired beauty, Lola was used to a lot of attention. She clearly hated sharing the limelight with her beau's sister. Almost before the last notes of Ariadne's song had faded, she spoke up. "Some people jes' love that kinda opera, don't they, but it's not everybody's cup of tea."

Stanley turned to her, with a tiny smile on his lips. "No? Not *your* cup of tea?"

"Me? I much prefer the music that comes outta the hills of the South. Ever hear of the Grand Ole Opry?"

Everyone fell silent. Not one of us, it seems, had ever heard of the Grand Ole Opry. Lola's eyes brightened as she surveyed the room and saw everyone looking at her. "It's real popular where I come from. And it's real gen-u-wine, too." Her eyes slid towards Ariadne to see how her competitor would react.

Ariadne didn't seem to notice, she stood up and graciously asked, "Who would like a slice of lemon cake?" Then she glanced shyly at Stanley. "It's my only contribution to this fantastic meal."

Stanley winked back. "If you never baked a cake in your life, honey, you'd still be the sweetest gal alive." The two gazed at one another adoringly.

I glanced at Lola and saw her lips press tightly together. Twice this evening, she'd lost everyone's attention. For the moment she was quelled, but I could imagine her plotting to regain our attention, no matter what it took.

When Arabella and I finally crawled into our beds hours later, I said, "This house seems awfully small for two very forceful women." To me, it seemed as if a cosmic struggle between these two Amazon queens might erupt any minute.

"Oh no! They get along great," Arabella purred. "So do Uncle Diego and Stanley." She lay back on the bed, a dreamy look on her face. "I doubt any girl in the world could have a more marvelous family! Don't you agree?" My dear friend was so happy at that instant, I hated to express any doubt. Still, my gut was warning me—trouble might be heading our way.

CHAPTER THIRTEEN

Time seemed to swim by at Arabella's house. There were so many people in one house, you were always running into someone. And that also meant there was always something to do and someone to do it with. Ariadne didn't like being still for long; she loved to plan activities. "Let's all go for a picnic in the woods," she'd announce.

"But it snowed a few days ago," Arabella would protest. "And the snow will be a foot deep in the woods."

"Then we'll bring along snowshoes," her mother would respond.

Whatever she proposed, no matter how impractical, Stanley would agree to do it. We had picnics in the snow. We ice skated on a pond in the forest. We jumped in the automobile to visit nearby towns like Albuquerque or Taos, sometimes driving for hours.

Whatever plan Ariadne suggested, Lola found an excuse not to participate. She was tired, she needed to take a bath, or she had to go shopping. Of course (though we protested to the contrary), none of us really missed her company. As for Uncle Diego, he rarely joined us, either, because he was busy in his studio painting.

So it was just the four of us on outings. We laughed at Stanley's corny jokes, listened to Ariadne's arias, and ate hot dogs and burgers and burritos and tamales and piñon nuts— whatever we could find in any picturesque diner along the way.

If not for all the new soldiers in town, it would have been hard to believe a war was going on. But there were servicemen everywhere. It seemed as if every young man in New Mexico had signed up. And the local population cheered them on. Even so, the news about the New Mexican troops in the Philippines was never good. It was a like a dark cloud hovering in the clear deep blue sky above.

When I managed to speak to Esteban about his cousins, his face would turn grim. And he'd shake his head sadly.

Every Friday I received a letter from Clem. She wasn't particularly happy either. "We're drowning in paperwork," she claimed. "Yards and yards of it. I have yet to train one nurse, but I've filled out forms by the hundreds." She also described the difficulty of finding a place to live. "I jump up at 5:00 a.m. and start looking at the classifieds in the *Washington Post*. But whenever I call about a place, somebody's always beat me to the punch. People must stay up all night." She was still sleeping on someone's sofa and barely found time to eat. "Managed a ham sandwich or two today. Sure miss Dolores's cooking. She's going to have to send me some green chile."

I wrote back regularly. But, in view of her difficulties, I hated to describe all the fun we were having. Also I feared it might be too much fun for Arabella. When I had arrived from England, I had been substantially ahead academically. Harrington Junior High School was a *breeze*, as Americans liked to describe anything particularly easy. But Arabella had never been particularly focused on schoolwork. Now she was having a very difficult time—she was close to failing geography and geometry. Math had always been her weakest subject.

One afternoon, she was seated at the dining room table, poring over the geometry textbook. She looked especially downcast.

"Want some help?" I offered.

She shook her head. "I just need to do these forty problems." She stared down at the paper in misery. "I don't want Hank to think I'm stupid."

"Hank? Is he the only reason you don't want to fail geometry?"

Arabella shrugged. "Honestly, when would I ever use geometry? Ariadne can't measure the radius of a circle. Stanley doesn't know the formula for an isosceles triangle. And they both do fine."

"So maybe Hank doesn't care what you know either." I shook my head. I hated for my best friend to sound like a simpleton.

"Oh no. Hank wants to become a scientist. I've heard him say so—a biologist or a chemist or a phy-phys-something. If he thinks I'm stupid, he'll never, never...well, you see how much he talks to that girl, Esther Wieden?" She gazed at me desperately. "I can't even guess what they talk about." Still wretched, she buried her head back in the geometry book.

I tried to sound sympathetic. "Once you catch on, geometry

is pretty neat. I love how the formulas for the size of circles and triangles work out so perfectly."

Arabella looked up at me dubiously. "They don't work out for me."

That afternoon I couldn't bear her self-pity a moment longer. So I fled the house. It was almost four. But the days now were growing a trifle longer and I still had some afternoon ahead of me. As I strolled downtown, gray clouds scooted across the sky. A chilly wind blew in fits and starts. I looked to see if Esteban was anywhere on the Plaza. Not glimpsing him, I decided to head toward Zook's Pharmacy. Perhaps Francis was reading comics. I'd only gone a few steps, however, when I spied Miss White. She was standing outside a store, gazing at some large Indian pots displayed in the window. Thinking this might be a good time to talk with her, I drew near.

"Hello, Miss White?" She didn't immediately respond. When she did look up at me, her eyes were a bit misty.

"Beautiful, aren't they?" she murmured.

"The pots?" I said.

She nodded. "That's the reason Martha and I came here twenty years ago. We fell in love with...with the beauty." She became silent again. I wanted to know who Martha was but thought it might be rude to ask.

Without her giant dogs at her side, she looked fragile and rather lonely. "Would you like a cup of tea?" she asked suddenly.

Her suggestion took me by surprise. And yet the idea of a cup of hot tea seemed irresistible. "Yes, please," I said. "I'd like that very much."

She started to walk at such a quick pace, I had to hurry

to keep up. "When I first arrived in Santa Fe, there was no place to get a cup of good tea," she explained. "So I created a tea shop." A tea shop? Really? I could hardly wait to discover where it was.

We walked from the Plaza up Palace Avenue. This long street commenced downtown and slowly wound eastward up a hill lined with big, beautiful houses.

After only a block or two, Miss White ducked into a door on the left and I followed. Inside was a large patio ringed with two-story buildings like an old Mexican hacienda. The small open plaza was filled with trees and bushes. "My goodness," I exclaimed, looking around. "It must be beautiful here in the spring and summer."

"Indeed, it is very lovely." She smiled and gestured to a doorway. "Here we are." We entered a little shop. There was a counter where tea was sold and several small tables. Miss White spoke to the clerk, who was dressed neatly in a little uniform with an apron. "Mildred, I believe this young lady would like some excellent English tea. Could you prepare a pot for us, please?"

The woman gave a small curtsy. "Of course, Miss White."

The two of us sat down at a table. A moment later, Mildred brought over a tray with exquisite tea cups, a little pot of tea, a small pitcher of cream, and several biscuits. How extraordinary! Real English tea in the middle of Santa Fe. How was it I had never even heard of the tearoom? Who did know about it? Only Miss White and her friends? It was like a secret tearoom within a secret garden. How strange and yet how sweet!

We sipped in silence for a moment. We both were enjoying the simple pleasure of good hot tea and real cream. Finally, mustering some courage, I broached the subject of my idea. "Excuse me, but I wonder if you saw in the newspaper how they're creating a group called Dogs for Defense," I explained. "They particularly want large dogs, so I thought of your—"

"Oh yes, Dogs for Defense," said Miss White. "I'm the president of the New Mexico Kennel Club so, naturally, they approached me about heading up the effort."

"You're in ch-charge?" I stammered.

"I didn't want to be, but no one else, well, no one else was quite up to the job."

"What is the job? What will you do?"

"You've met Alex, of course. Mr. Scott will train the animals. He's learning how to do that now. As you can imagine, training a dog to appear in a dog show is quite different from training them for battle." She sighed. "I saw the military dogs in Belgium, where I served as a volunteer for the Red Cross."

My eyes widened. "You were in the Red Cross during the Great War? Did you know Clem served there, too?"

Miss White turned her keen gaze toward me. "They're not calling it the Great War any more. It's now called the *First World War*, and what's happening now is being called the Second World War." She looked away. "I wonder if wars will ever end or if we'll have to endure a third and a fourth." Lifting the tea cup to her lips, her hand slightly trembled.

"I certainly hope they don't continue," I exclaimed. "But I do hope we beat the Nazis and the Imperial Japanese."

"I certainly hope so, too." She looked at me again and a tiny smile crossed her lips. "Yes, I did know that Miss Pope had served, although she was in France, while I was in Belgium. And she was trained as a real nurse, while I was simply a volunteer. But I'm sure we both saw enough horrors to know how awful war is. And we've never spoken of it to each other. Funny, but we've always had so much else to talk about—like Indian health care at the pueblos. We discuss what needs to be done now, not the past. That's the important thing."

"So, will your wolfhounds be part of Dogs for Defense?"

Miss White straightened up, proudly. "Of course, you saw Gareth and Zara. They'll be ideal for the job, so intelligent and faithful. But we need other dogs, too. The army would like to have thousands. And I'm not sure how to find any in Santa Fe."

I didn't hesitate a second. "There must be lots of capable dogs here. And I'd be happy to help locate them."

"Would you really?" She looked pleased. "How would you do that?"

"I don't yet know," I admitted. "But I'm sure to think of something soon." Then I added, "I promised Clem that I'd continue being helpful. And so far I haven't done a thing. Living with Arabella and her family is…well, it's rather distracting."

"No doubt." Miss White gave me a keen look as she drained the last of her tea. "I was planning to recruit several volunteer aids, perhaps you might consider…."

"Oh yes, of course," I piped up immediately. "That would be lovely. Anything at all I can do."

"Well, bring me your ideas for one."

I nodded, draining the last of my tea. It was so good, I wanted to relish every bit of the flavor. I glanced over at Miss White, recalling that I had chosen to stay with Arabella rather than with her. Had I hurt her feelings? If she minded, she didn't let on. She gestured to the woman behind the counter. "Mildred, could you please pack a tin of good English tea for this young lady to take with her?"

Mildred nodded curtly and started to prepare the tin. "This has been so pleasant, Miss White," I said quickly. "Thank you so very much."

She gazed at me thoughtfully a moment and then stood up and gathered her purse. "It's been a pleasant afternoon for me, too. I don't always…," her voice faltered for a second. "Well, I enjoyed your company very much."

As we walked out of the shop, I must say that her step seemed firmer and her eyes clearer and brighter. Was it simply my company she'd so enjoyed? Or the possibility we might work together soon on an important project for the American military? Either way, I was pleased.

CHAPTER FOURTEEN

All that evening, I pondered how I could help with Dogs for Defense. Arabella was still attempting to study geometry—though she complained as much as she studied. And every thirty minutes, she claimed she required *une divertissement*, otherwise she'd absolutely go bananas. (Sprinkling her vocabulary with French expressions was a bit of an affectation Arabella had picked up from Ariadne.) Her distractions included fixing a giant bowl of buttered popcorn; playing with her mother's Siamese cats, Major and Minor, and flipping through old issues of *Harper's Bazaar*.

I must have looked dubious about the value of the fashion magazine. "You think I'm wasting my time?" she said, hotly defending herself. "It says right here that this is a magazine for the well-dressed woman with the well-dressed mind." She gazed at me confidently. "That's who I intend to be."

As she stroked the cats, I developed an idea for promoting Dogs for Defense: posters. I'd create a poster and then put them all over town, requesting that people submit their pet dogs. Alex Scott would determine if each dog was suitable to serve in the army.

I described the project to the whole household at dinner. It was 9:00 p.m. by the time Stanley had finished baking a large casserole of beef stroganoff. He spooned the creamy meat and noodles onto our plates with great pride. By then, I was so starving I probably could have devoured shoe leather. Still, the stroganoff was absolutely the most delicious thing I'd ever put in my mouth.

"That's a good idea," said Uncle Diego, referring to the project. "But what will the poster look like?"

"Very simple," I replied. "I will state that the U.S. Army needs dogs and list the place to take the dog and other relevant information."

He shook his head. "No one will even look at a poster like that. People like pictures—you must put a picture of a dog on it."

"What a great idea," exclaimed Lola. "And you're such a talented artist, why don't you paint a picture of a dog?"

"Yes, Diego," said Ariadne with the mischievous look of a younger sister. "That could be your contribution to the war effort."

Uncle Diego frowned. Before Pearl Harbor, he had claimed to be a pacifist, someone who's against all wars, no matter what. Since the Japanese assault on Pearl Harbor, he'd reluctantly suggested that this particular war might be necessary. But he hated all the gung-ho celebrations to encourage young men to sign up. "People won't be cheering in a year or two when the telegrams start to arrive. There'll be a lot of grieving families in this town."

Now he simply stated, "I'm a painter. I don't do commercial art. If I start decorating posters or brochures, everybody in town would want one. I'd have no time for my own paintings." He turned to me. "Find an amateur artist, a beginner. It doesn't need to be a great picture. Just so it looks like a dog."

I couldn't help grinning; I knew just whom to ask.

The following day at lunch, I sought out Francis. "I'm wondering if you could help me?"

His eyes narrowed. "What do you want?"

"A picture of a dog. Could you draw one?" I described the Dogs for Defense project to him. "Maybe," he muttered. "If I can find the time."

Francis was an odd fellow. Sometimes he seemed quite friendly. Other times he'd ignore me completely. But this day, he trotted over as soon as the final school bell rang. He stared at me a moment, then burst out, "C-can you come to my house?" His face was pink with excitement. "I've got drawing supplies there. I could draw a couple of pictures, and you could choose the one you like."

"Where do you live?" I asked.

"On Griffin Street, close to the train station. Know where that is?"

I nodded. Arabella and I had traipsed far and wide around the town. But we didn't usually go near the train station. Passenger trains (like the one I had arrived on or that Clem had departed on) stopped twenty miles from Santa Fe, in the village of Lamy. Only freight trains came all the way to Santa Fe— hauling coal and lumber and machinery. The surrounding neighborhood wasn't particularly pleasant. Sometimes hobos, hopping on and off the freight trains, lingered in that part of town.

I thought hard a moment. Should I go with Francis to his house? Was it safe? Was it proper? I knew it was terribly poor etiquette for a young lady to visit a young man's house unchaperoned. My Great-Aunt Augusta would be scandalized. I could almost hear her stentorian voice: "For goodness sake, Beatrice, you do know better."

On the other hand, my great-aunt was far, far away in England. This was the United States of America—a very different sort of place with different rules. Besides, I figured, a thirteen-year-old, who'd traveled across the Atlantic on her own, should be able to walk a few blocks. "Yes, I'll come, Francis," I replied decisively.

A look of pleasure washed across his face.

I had one question. "Are you sure your uncle won't mind?"

He hesitated a split-second. "Don't worry. He won't be there. He's real busy right now. Got a new job fixing up an old army camp." So that afternoon the two of us walked to his house. Unlike other times that we'd been together, Francis opened up and chattered the whole way.

I learned that his mother worked at a munitions factory in San Diego. Most of the workers were women—they were making weapons for the war. She hadn't worked before, but now she was "happy as a clam" and making a pile of money. "Plus, she's made a lot of girlfriends," he explained. "They do stuff together after work."

A shadow passed over his face. "I think she was glad to see me go. Easier with no kid to care for, you know?"

I glanced over. How awful for him to think that his mother

was *glad* for him to leave. Before I could say anything, however, he rattled on. "It's okay. Me and my dad are super pals." His eyes lit up. "We used to do stuff together like build model planes, and we had a fantastic train set." His face fell. "Mom sold it soon as Dad shipped out. Said it was babyish to have a train set. When I said Dad liked it, too, she said, 'Yeah, well, your father just never could grow up.'"

By then we were on Griffin Street. In the middle of the block, he pointed to a shabby little house in a dirt yard. It had only one tree stuck in the middle, with a scrawny black dog tied to it.

The poor animal barked loudly as we approached. It certainly wasn't suited, either physically or temperamentally, for the U.S. Canine Corps.

Seeing his home, my heart sank. No wonder Francis looked so pinched and unhappy. For someone who wanted to be an artist, living in such an ugly and forlorn place must be miserable. As if guessing my thoughts, he paused before opening the gate. "It was really nice for you to come. I didn't think you would."

Then he opened the gate and went to untie the dog. "Here, Champ. Here, ole fella." The dog immediately scampered in circles around his feet, half-crazed with gratitude. When we went in the house, Champ eagerly followed.

The rooms were nearly empty, with a few pieces of rickety furniture. The dull grayish-green walls were bare. There was no warmth or color at all. Then Francis led me to his room. How different! The floor was covered by a bright flowered rug. "Somebody down the street threw this out," he announced proudly. "I just had to clean it." On the wall hung a huge map of the world, stippled with different-colored push-pins. He explained that he was following the progress of the war. Red pins were the primary Axis Powers—Germany, Italy, and Japan—while blue pins signified the major Allies—the United States and Great Britain.

"I wish I knew exactly where Dad's ship is—I could stick a pin there. But he can't tell the location—it's secret." He stared gloomily at the great blue expanse of Pacific Ocean. "He could be anywhere."

"Where's Pearl Harbor?" I asked, peering at the map. He pointed to a blue pin stuck on a tiny island. How forlorn it looked – in the middle of that vast blueness. I also wanted to see where Manila and the Philippine Islands were. Francis pointed to a a string of islands much farther west. A yellow pin had been stuck next to a blue pin. "The United States still has air bases there, but the Japs have been bombing the heck out of 'em. So I don't know which pin to stick in there right now."

I was very impressed by how much Francis knew. Behind his unfortunate appearance was a very clever brain. "Lots of those soldiers come from New Mexico," I murmured. Seeing the map, I realized how very far from home they were. "It must be awful."

"Yeah, I know." Then Francis fell silent a moment, looking uneasy. When he finally spoke, his voice was low and tense. "Hey, wanna know a secret? A big secret?"

I hesitated, unsure if I did want to know. But he didn't wait. "I told you my uncle was working on an old military camp. You know why?"

I shook my head and he continued, "They're fixing it up to stick Japanese people there. They're bringing them on the train from California and Oregon and Washington state. Hundreds, maybe thousands."

I recalled what Clem had said weeks before. Still his news took me by surprise. "Really? They're really coming to Santa Fe?"

He nodded. "They're taking them off the West Coast. They say the Japanese in the U.S. might send signals to the Japanese in Japan. Or help them invade somehow." Francis seemed unhappy. "What do you think? A lot of these Japanese are American citizens. They're not Japanese citizens. Why would they help the enemy?"

"I don't know," I murmured, thinking hard. "I suppose it's better to be safe than sorry." It seemed like a weak answer.

"Maybe." He hesitated before speaking. "But there were a lot of Japanese people living near us in San Diego. Some of them were…they were really nice." His gaze dropped to his hands, he bit his lower lip and he picked at a thumbnail.

I remembered what Stanley had said about Japanese shopkeepers being trustworthy. Then I thought of what Donald had said about them being sneaky. *Maybe it only required a few bad apples…*that a popular American expression–perhaps it applied here. Who was right? How could you know? It seemed as if wartime had made such decisions far more difficult. As if ordinary 'rights' and 'wrongs' had flipped and become all topsy-turvy.

In any case, Francis seemed eager to change the subject. Looking up again, he said quickly, "Hey, let's get started. I can draw the dog while you print out the words."

We worked for about an hour or more. He sketched a number of pictures using the little dog Champ for a model. Not that the dog would stay still. He nervously ran in and out of the room and in circles around the room. But Francis didn't seem to mind. He drew one picture after another, studied each, and then balled it up and tossed it in the corner.

"Why are you throwing them away?" I finally asked. "They look good to me."

He shook his head. "Nah, not good enough." He lifted his chin. "Not for a *real* artist."

I glanced out the window; the light was growing dim. "Well, I have to leave now." I showed him what I'd written. "As soon as you draw a picture you like, we'll take this stuff to the printer and get the posters made," I said. "Then we'll put them up all over town."

"All over town? My pictures all over town?" He grinned, his eyes shone.

It was the first time I'd seen Francis happy.

CHAPTER FIFTEEN

Francis walked me to the gate outside. "Would you like me to walk you home?"

I was pleased—what a gentleman. But I shook my head. "Oh no, it's not so far. And I know the way better than you do." Yet walking down Griffin Street, I realized that it was nearly dark. I had rarely been so far from home by myself. I quickened my pace, but in the dim light it was hard to see. First I nearly stumbled on a curb, then almost smacked into a tall, thin man.

He stopped short, speaking brusquely. "Who are you? Vat are you doing here?" His voice had a distinct accent.

"I'm…I'm just heading home," I replied.

"You lif near here?" He glanced around the neighborhood. Lit only by a streetlamp, the houses appeared poor and seedy.

"No, I…I live across town." Why was he so curious?

He studied me closer. "Why, you haf a British accent." A corner of his mouth turned up, but it wasn't reassuring. "Far from your real home, aren't you?'"

Somehow his gaze made me uncomfortable. "You aren't American either," I replied quickly. "Where are you from?"

He hesitated a second. "Switzerland." Only he said it like *Svit-zar-lanndt*.

Of course. Now I remembered. He was the man I had seen on the Plaza that afternoon with Clem—the one reading the newspaper. Switzerland, I knew, was divided into three parts. And in each part, the people spoke a different language: French, Italian, and German. But his accent wasn't French or Italian, it was definitely German. I looked at him more closely. His face would have been handsome if the features had lined up evenly. Instead, he had a sharp, edgy look with small, light-blue eyes and longish, very blond hair.

"Vell, little girl, you should hurry home now." He studied me another moment, then doffed his hat. "It's not gutt to be out after dark. You might run into someone who's not so nice az me." With a final sharp glance in my direction, he walked on, and I noticed he had a slight limp.

I didn't waste an instant. I took off, first walking fast, then nearly running in my haste. For the first time since her departure, I felt Clem's absence keenly. I felt alone and...and unprotected.

Fifteen minutes later, breathless, I flung open the door of Arabella's house. Ariadne saw me first. "My goodness, Beatrice. We were just looking for you."

"You-you were?" I stammered. "Well, I...I went to a friend's house to, to..."

Ariadne seemed completely unconcerned, as if it barely mattered where I'd been. "You had a telephone call a short while ago," she interrupted. "I'll get you the number."

"A telephone call? For me?" In all my time in the United States, I'd only received a handful of calls. On my birthday, my parents had gone to great trouble and expense to make a trans-Atlantic telephone call. The line was so poor, however, I could barely hear their voices. And I had cried for hours afterward, realizing how much I missed them.

Ariadne handed me a message: *Please call Alex Scott at 3432.*

Oh my goodness—how perfect! I needed Mr. Scott's number to put on the Dogs for Defense poster. I hurried to phone him.

It cheered me to no end to hear his hearty Scottish voice. "Miss Sims, I wonder if you'd care to join me on a ride Saturday morning, when I take the hounds out for a run?"

I nearly jumped up and down with excitement. "I'd love to go, of course."

"Then we'll have a horse all saddled and ready for you. Be here by eight."

I put down the phone. I loved horses and I loved riding. But the only riding I'd done in New Mexico had been with Esteban. We'd ridden bareback on sturdy Indian ponies, using only a rope bridle. I suspected Saturday's outing would be quite different.

And aside from the horses, there'd be those fantastic dogs! I looked forward to learning more about them and seeing them loose in the countryside.

Later that night, Arabella and I lay in our beds talking. I told her about the afternoon's adventures. How Francis lived in a sad, little house. About the dog Champ and the pictures Francis drew rapidly, one after another. "He's quite talented. I just hope he is satisfied with one of his pictures, so we can use it for a poster!"

I hesitated for a moment and then spoke in a hushed voice. I told her about coming home at dusk and meeting the strange man from Switzerland. Recalling his sharp face and German accent was unsettling.

"Switzerland?" said Arabella. "It's a neutral country, isn't it? Not on the Nazi German side or on the US-British side of the war?"

"That's right, it's neutral," I replied. "They say there are people so desperate to leave Nazi Germany, they walk across the high Swiss mountains covered in snow. Men and women and even little children walk for days, hoping reach safety."

"How awful! I couldn't walk even one mile across snowy mountains," said Arabella.

"Then the Nazis would shoot you."

"Heavens! What a choice." Her eyes grew big, just imagining. "I hope we beat the Nazis soon."

I sighed, rolling back over and gazing at the ceiling. "Me too. And maybe it will happen now that the Americans and British are fighting together."

"I wonder who that man was. He told you he's Swiss, but you say his accent is German," muttered Arabella. "Maybe he's really German but doesn't want you to know."

Suddenly my skin felt goose-bumpy. "Why would he not want me to know?" Then my brain cells caught fire. "You think he might be a spy?" I gasped. In England, I had seen numerous posters about the danger of spies. "Careless talk costs lives" was a slogan everyone knew.

"It's possible. That's why they're rounding up the Japanese

people. They think some of them might be spies."

I fell silent a moment. I was dying to tell her that the rumors were true. There were Japanese coming to Santa Fe! But Francis had said it was a secret, so I resisted. "I wonder how can you tell if someone is a spy or not?"

"I bet it's not that hard." Arabella sounded impatient. "I bet if you look a person straight in the eye and they can't look you back, fair and square, they're probably a spy."

"You sound like Donald Riggsbee," I said. "He always thinks he knows who's bad or who's good with just one look."

Arabella giggled. "You're right. That is something he'd say." She paused a moment. "You know what he says about Francis?"

I shook my head, expecting the worst.

"He says he's a loony. That he doesn't belong in a normal school with regular kids like us." She tossed her red curls back off her face. "He can't imagine why you'd want to spend any time with him." She gazed at me fondly. "I told him to stuff it —you could be friends with anyone you want."

Arabella was a true pal. But even she didn't truly understand why I was befriending Francis. Closing my eyes I could see the little house in the dirt lot. Poor boy, thinking his mother didn't care for him and not knowing where his beloved father was. Why, he couldn't even stick a pin in the spot. Francis hardly seemed better off than his poor dog, tied to a tree all day, barking.

Then I recalled his smile on being asked to participate in this project. He'd do an excellent job with the drawing. I knew he would!

The following day, Francis rushed up to me at lunchtime, his eyes bright. "Let's go someplace where we can look at these," he whispered secretively, indicating a large manila envelope.

"All right," I said, looking around. I was following Arabella to a table in the cafeteria. But she wouldn't miss me for a few minutes. We probably spent too much time together, anyway.

"Let's go to the library," Francis said. "It's quiet now. Miss Tingley just sits at her desk, eating her sandwich and reading the newspaper." I guessed that was where Francis spent his time when he disappeared from the cafeteria. We weren't supposed to have food in there but Miss Tingley, with her round spectacles and frizzy grey hair, probably had a soft spot for oddballs like Francis.

A few minutes later, we were both seated at one of the large library tables. Francis slid three pictures of Champ out of the envelope. In one, the little dog was running out the door. In another, he was sitting with begging eyes, as if waiting for a treat. In the third, he was lying on his back with his paws in the air, wanting to be scratched.

I studied the pictures. Francis was holding his breath, waiting for me to speak. "They're all extremely good." I said finally, glancing at him. "Don't you think?"

He smiled a bit. "They're okay."

"No, quite honestly, I've seen a fair number of paintings of dogs—London museums are full of them. And I've rarely seen any that are better than these." Actually, I was exaggerating a little, because I'd only seen dogs a few times in pictures. They were usually fox hounds, poised at the foot of horses, ready to go on a hunt.

But Francis clearly believed me. "Really?"

"Well, you haven't worked in oils yet, but I'm sure you will one day," I said with great solemnity. "And then, who knows, one of your paintings might hang in a museum."

Francis stared at me, speechless. The idea had obviously never crossed his mind. In fact, he was probably quite content to dream of drawing for comic books.

"I suppose you want me to choose one for the poster?" I said quickly.

He nodded, his eyes big. It was a serious moment. Which would I choose?

"Well, I like them all. But for our purposes, I think this one is most suitable." I pointed to the seated dog with begging eyes. "He's almost saying, 'I belong in the army, don't I?'"

Francis picked up that drawing and looked at it closely. Then he looked back at me. "Yeah, you're right. This one will be best."

"But if you don't mind giving up another, I'd love to hang one of them in my room. And I'm sure Arabella would be pleased, too."

Francis turned to me, stunned. "Sure, I guess, yeah, why not?" he stumbled through a litany of replies. "Which do you want?"

I decided quickly because I was getting hungry. "The running one," I said. "He looks like he's going somewhere important."

Francis started to hand it to me and then pulled it back. "I bet you want me to sign it."

I smiled. "Of course."

So he added his name at the bottom with a flourish. Maybe

he had envisioned himself as a grand artist, after all. With the two pictures in hand, I headed back to the lunchroom. Francis said he'd remain in the library. I think he wanted to sit and savor his success a while longer.

That afternoon, we took the picture and text to the printer. The man in charge was extremely helpful in assembling the poster. We said we wanted about twenty-five copies. He told us they'd be ready by Monday. Then Francis and I celebrated our accomplishment at Zook's.

Naturally, I had another good excuse for why I should pay for his ice-cream sundae. "It's only fair, since you've given me such a fine drawing," I explained. Watching him slurp up the vanilla ice cream and hot butterscotch sauce, I wondered if either of his parents had ever bought him a sundae.

CHAPTER SIXTEEN

The following day was Saturday. When I climbed out of my bed, Arabella was still snoring. It was not surprising, since the night before we hadn't eaten until after 10:00 p.m. That's when Stanley had served his delicious Greek moussaka—a delectable combination of sliced eggplant, ground beef and cheesy cream sauce. After the meal, Ariadne had entertained us with arias until nearly midnight—all of us, that is, except Lola, who excused herself saying she had a headache.

After such a celebration, I assumed everyone in the household would stay fast asleep until much later in the morning. I tiptoed through the house, carrying my riding boots. When I entered the kitchen, however, Uncle Diego was standing at the window, stirring a cup of coffee. He was still wearing his flannel pajamas and a ratty, old tartan robe. Lola complained often and loudly about the condition of his bathrobe, saying he should replace it with a new one. But Uncle Diego was equally adamant about retaining this one. "I have a long history with this bathrobe," he claimed. "I know every spot and hole in it and that's very meaningful to me."

Hearing me enter, he now turned around. "Going out, Beatrice? Better dress warmly, we could get some bad weather."

"Oh dear." I glanced out the window as I pulled on the boots. It did seem a little gray and forbidding but, perhaps, it would clear up later. I certainly didn't want bad weather to spoil my ride.

Uncle Diego eyed me with a bit of a smile. "Looks like you're going someplace special?"

"Alex Scott has invited me to ride with him and the wolfhounds," I responded, breaking into a grin. I couldn't help feeling elegant as I spun around to proudly show off my outfit. I was wearing beige riding jodhpurs, a tattersall shirt that tied in a bow at the neck, and short, brown riding boots. Absolutely the perfect attire for a young female equestrian. Yet the entire outfit had been folded neatly in the bottom of my trunk for over a year with no opportunity to wear it.

"Well, you better get going," said Uncle Diego. "And I hope the weather holds for you."

I assembled two peanut butter sandwiches, added a heavy jacket, and took off. I'd never seen or tasted peanut butter before coming to the United States. Now I considered it to be an indispensable invention. A few days earlier, Lola had claimed a Negro from her home state of Alabama had invented the peanut as well as peanut butter. Though she couldn't recall his name.

"His name is George Washington Carver," Stanley explained patiently. He always knew everything about food. "He didn't invent the peanut—that probably came from Africa.

But you're right, he did create peanut butter. A brilliant man."

"My, my, I won't forget that!" exclaimed Lola. Then she repeated his name slowly. "Ge-or-ge Wa-shing-ton Cah-vuh. " Arabella and I rolled our eyes. Lola was beginning to lose any charm she'd ever possessed in our view. She tried to take credit for nearly everything without ever complimenting anyone else.

Munching a peanut butter sandwich as I hurried to Miss White's house, however, I left behind any worries about our household. Glancing upward at the darkening sky, I also attempted to leave behind any concerns about the weather. It would be awful if today's outing were squashed.

But Alex Scott barely mentioned the weather. He was all ready to go, with two handsome horses saddled and bridled. The dogs were running in circles, eager to take off. Their large ears were slightly lifted, awaiting any word from Mr. Scott.

"Hallo there," he announced cheerfully. I wiped a few crumbs from my mouth and returned the greeting. "You seem all ready for our ride. Shouldn't be out more than an hour or two. And the storm is supposed to hold off until midday." He indicated a mounting stool. "Oh, I shan't need that," I declared proudly. When riding with Esteban, I had hauled myself up on the backs of ponies by gripping a piece of mane. Using the stirrup on a saddle to mount seemed far more simple.

Mr. Scott seemed impressed. He gestured to the delicate gray mare. "Gracie is quite lively, but not overly daring." Then he swung up on his large bay horse. "And Tim is a very reliable comrade."

Following a signal from Mr. Scott, the dogs took off, and we followed at a canter. We sped across the road and over the nearby hillside. We passed through short bushy piñon trees and evergreens at a fast clip. Then we slowed to dip into deep arroyos—the wide sandy ditches that filled with fast-flowing water during summer rainstorms. As we descended these slopes, I leaned far back in the saddle. Then as Gracie staggered back up the steep arroyo bank, I leaned forward so far forward my nose was tickled by her mane.

The wind had picked up, but the horses seemed to scarcely notice. The dogs also appeared to enjoy pressing forward at an easy lope or flat-out run. We rode higher and higher until Mr. Scott finally halted. "Look there," he commanded, pointing. I turned round in the saddle. Indeed, it was a beautiful view of the entire little town spread below us.

I could identify the big, golden sandstone cathedral, St. Francis, a block from the Plaza. Other steeples were also visible. There was the cross atop San Miguel Chapel, a simple sanctuary constructed entirely of mud adobe and reputed to be the oldest church in the West.

I was still admiring the view when, all of a sudden, we heard a loud yelping. Two of the younger dogs, Loppy and Gelert, had gone off in pursuit of a stray coyote. Now both had returned, but one was limping badly and yelping.

"That rascal, Loppy—he led off the youngster and now Gelert's hurt." He swung out of his saddle. "I best tend to the pup now." Gelert had dropped to the ground and was diligently licking his back leg and paw. The other dogs drew around in a circle. They watched as Mr. Scott knelt down and examined the wound.

"What is it?" I called to him. "What's wrong?"

"A clean cut—must have been some broken glass. Damn people come up here to drink beer, and the miserable sods break their bottles." He was furious. And I guessed his fury hid his worry. "It's deep enough, the poor tyke shouldn't walk farther. Not without a proper dressing. And I don't have a stout enough bandage that will stick on for our return."

He stood up, hands on hips. "In an hour or so, I could bring the vet up here. If I can find him quick. But I hate to leave the dog alone, even a short while."

That's when I heard a clear, steady voice say, "I'll stay with him. I don't mind a bit." And I realized it was my own.

"Oh no, lassie, you couldn't." He almost smiled, clearly appreciating the offer. "It'll be some time 'til I can locate the man and get him back here. And lookee there." He pointed to the grey clouds now rushing toward us. "No telling what that's going to bring with it."

As if in answer, a light flurry of snow began falling. Though only a few flakes were drifting down at present, it promised to get heavier soon. The dogs moved restlessly.

"It will be all right. I've got my horse to keep me warm." My words sounded far more brave than I felt. Yet once I had spoken them, I believed I could stay and would stay and even desired to stay. To prove it to him and to myself, I climbed off Gracie and tethered her reins to the branch of a piñon. Then I casually leaned back against her warm, furry side, like I did this sort of thing every day.

Mr. Scott gazed at me a long moment while considering everything. "All right then, lassie, if you believe you can do it. I thank you kindly. I'll leave two of the older dogs with you." He spoke firmly but gently to Zara and Edain. The two lay down on either side of the hurt youngster. He glanced up at me. "They'll do their part. You need only keep watch." Then he climbed back on his horse. "I'm taking off this instant. And I'll be back quick as a man can."

Kicking Timothy hard, he seemed to fly down the hillside with the other eight dogs racing behind. It was only in this moment that I totally realized what I'd said I would do. Aside from the town far below us, there was no habitation in sight. No smoke curling up from a chimney, no noise from human or vehicle. Nothing but me and the wind and the occasional yelp from the poor hurt dog.

CHAPTER SEVENTEEN

The snow had begun falling heavily. There was already a thin layer covering the ground and the three dogs. I went over to them and flicked snow off their coats. Zara looked up at me gratefully with her beautiful deep-hazel eyes and licked my hand. But she didn't budge. I felt that nothing in the world would cause her to move, once Mr. Scott had bid her stay. Nothing.

Already I could see little of the town below. I could barely make out the steep roof of Loretto Chapel, an exquisite Gothic church, used by the girls who attended the Loretto Academy. Arabella knew several of the students and we had visited there during the Christmas festivities. The chapel walls had been lit by flickering candles and a choir of girls, almost invisible in the wooden gallery above, filled the sanctuary with their lilting voices.

My recollections were suddenly interrupted, however, when Zara raised her head, sniffed the air, and faintly growled.

I whipped around, expecting a bear or even a mountain lion. Instead, I saw a man cresting the ridge not a hundred feet away. He was dressed in khaki trousers and a heavy jacket. A rifle was slung over one shoulder, and a large pair of binoculars hung around his neck.

My first reaction was to call out to him. It would be such a relief to have some company in this remote spot. Yet something in his gait caused me to pause. He had a slight limp. As he neared, I could see him more clearly. Oh my gosh, I gasped, how was it possible? Here was the man I had met the other night. The man with the foreign accent who claimed to be Swiss.

He had spotted me as well and was heading my way.

I tried to think fast. What was he doing in the hills above the city? He was carrying a rifle and binoculars. Had he come to this excellent viewing site to spy on the town? And did he carry a rifle to shoot anyone who discovered him? Even someone as totally innocent and helpless as I?

"Vat's happening here?" he called out, coming up close. Gracie pawed the snowy ground. The dogs hadn't budged, but Zara was whining as if she were chained and wished she could be loosed. She clearly wanted to stand and protect us all. But she was bound to remain lying down by Mr. Scott's command.

"A hurt dog," I murmured.

"Is dat so?" He looked concerned. "They're Miss White's wolfhounds, aren't they?"

I nodded.

"An excellent breed for hunting."

"Hunting?"

He nodded. "Indeed. I'm a hunter, and I lead people on

hunts. I was just scouting this area to see if there's any game."

"In the middle of the winter?" My voice must have sounded doubtful.

"It's possible. A bear that gets hungry and climbs out of its den. Maybe an elk or mountain goat comes down from the mountains to feed. Anyway, I like to stay in shape." He looked at me keenly. "Why are you here with Miss White's dogs?" He put his hand out to feel the falling snow. "In a blizzard."

"It's not a blizzard *yet*," I said, as much to comfort myself as to inform him. "And I'm…I'm just guarding the dogs. Mr. Scott will be back soon."

"Hmm, maybe I should wait with you."

"No need for that," I said hastily. "He'll be back in…in minutes."

Perhaps I didn't sound convincing, for he didn't withdraw. "This seems a good spot to rest a bit." He rested his gun butt on the ground and indicated his binoculars. "Though not much of a day to view the city," he said smiling.

It certainly wasn't, I thought. Not a good day for hunting or for spying on the city either. So what was he really doing in this remote spot? Meeting another spy? My stomach quaked. What if there were two spies, and I learned of their existence? Then they'd have to get rid of me, wouldn't they?

I tried to think up an excuse to leave. I yearned to climb back on Gracie and gallop down the hill. Yet I knew I couldn't. Not after swearing to Mr. Scott that I'd stay with the dogs. In any case, I could barely see twenty feet ahead. I might lose my way in the snow. I knew I was stuck here until Mr. Scott returned.

Oh dear, that might be a problem as well. Shouldn't I

somehow warn Mr. Scott that we had an unwelcome visitor? That's what people did in the murder mysteries I had read. They figured out a way to warn others in advance of possible danger. I tried to come up with a plan, but my brain felt quite muddled, like a small child's, not a mature thirteen-year-old's. Clem said I had plenty of common sense, but I feared every morsel had momentarily fled.

Even with my warm jacket, the cold was pressing in hard. I yearned to be in a warm, safe place with a cup of hot tea or a mug of cocoa. With someone I knew well—with anyone, in fact—except this strange man.

"Perhaps I should introduce myself," said the Swiss man. "My name is James Prestre. Vat is your name?"

I'm not sure why I decided to give him a false name. After all, I had nothing to hide, but I said, "Gracie. Gracie Sims."

His mouth slid into a sort of crooked smile. "Do you have a special interest in dogs, Miss Sims?" He gestured to the wolfhounds still lying calmly nearby.

"Dogs?" I murmured uneasily, glancing at the three animals. I certainly didn't want to say anything about the Dogs for Defense. Wasn't that just the sort of thing a spy would want to know? How the enemy was preparing for war? The location and quantity of its canine forces?

A shudder of horror ran through me, and I reached over and put my hand on Zara.

"I see you do like dogs," said Mr. Prestre.

"Oh yes, I do," I said, nervously adding, "I had a little dog, Alfie, back in London. A Yorkshire terrier—so sweet, I miss him dreadfully."

"Toy dogs! Useless little things," he sneered. "In my profession, we use dogs for hunting, tracking. They have such excellent noses, they can track any sort of animal. Even human animals."

I could feel my eyes bulge. *Human animals?* Dogs tracking human animals? I hated how that sounded. "But... but you don't have a dog now?" I stammered.

"No, that is very sad. I could not bring my dog with me to this country. It's too bad. Wolfgang had an excellent nose and could track anything." He eyed the wolfhounds again. "Maybe I should get one here."

Not a chance, I thought, you certainly won't get one of Miss White's dogs. If anyone gets one, it will be the U.S. Army. The coats of the dogs were dusted with snow again. I wiped some off. Yet they didn't seem to even notice the cold. And now that they'd grown used to Mr. Prestre, they lay as calmly as before. Though Gelert never ceased licking his paw.

The two of us fell silent a moment. In fact, I was starting to say, "Really, you don't need to stay. I'm quite capable of being here alone," when all the dogs suddenly looked alert, their ears raised. Gelert yipped cheerfully. At first, I saw nothing, but a a few seconds later, Mr. Scott's very welcome face emerged through the veil of falling snow. Behind him strode Mr. Tremble, the veterinarian, carrying a satchel of supplies. Mr. Scott's face was creased with worry as he hurried up to the dogs.

"Still right where I bade them stay," he remarked to Mr. Tremble with a hint of pride. "Marvelous dogs, they are." Mr. Tremble immediately knelt and began getting out his supplies to bandage Gelert's paw. The dog quit whimpering and seemed almost grateful for the attention.

Satisfied, Mr. Scott turned and spoke to me. "And you, lass, how has it been for you? Frightfully cold, isn't it? He brought over a thick blanket to wrap around my shoulders. Then he opened a thermos of tea. Steam spilled into the cold air as he poured the hot, milky tea into a cup. I gratefully grasped it and began to sip.

"How fine of you to stay here all alone," said Mr. Scott. "Shows your strong British backbone."

"Well, I wasn't quite alone," I started to say. Looking over the rim of the cup, however, I didn't see Mr. Prestre. Where had he gone? Amazed, I gazed all around, but he was nowhere in sight. He must have slipped away while we were watching the vet bandaging Gelert's paw. How peculiar.

"No, you weren't all alone, lassie. You had these fine dogs to keep you company." He stroked Gracie's neck. "And an excellent horse, as well. You couldn't do with much better company than that."

Hours later, I finally reached Arabella's house. By then, the snow was thickly blanketing the streets and houses. I felt fortunate to have made it back at all. Quickly undressing, I sank into a hot bath. The moment I climbed out, Arabella began hounding me with questions. She wanted to know everything.

"We didn't expect such a storm," I explained. "And we would have missed the worst of it if a dog hadn't gotten hurt. So Mr. Scott had to go for the vet, leaving me alone."

"Alone?" Arabella's mouth dropped open. "You were alone on the mountain?"

I nodded, quite matter-of-factly. "For a bit I was." Then I explained the mysterious appearance and disappearance of Mr. Prestre.

Arabella stared. "Mr. Prestre? The strange man who claims to be Swiss? How bizarre for you to meet him again." She gasped. "Human animals? Perhaps, he's tracking you!"

"Oh my God." The very idea made me me feel slightly nauseous and weak in the knees. I climbed on my bed and added crossly, "Do you mind leaving me a bit on my own? I really need a nap." Then I pulled a blanket over my head.

Arabella reluctantly left the room. Downstairs, Ariadne was exercizing her voice, filling the house with high notes. The covers weren't sufficient. Pulling the pillow from under my head, I stuck it over my head. And finally slept.

Hours later, Arabella roused me. Her face was pink from excitement and the heat of the kitchen. "Please come and eat! Stanley and I have prepared a masterpiece."

I pulled myself from under the covers. "All right." Suddenly I was ravenous.

Indeed, the Italian lasagna they put in the middle of the table was magnificent. The cheese and tomato sauce oozed and bubbled lusciously. I devoured my portion and asked for seconds and considered a third.

"You can have mine, sweetie, I could barely touch the stuff." Lola pushed her plate in my direction. It looked as if she'd only nibbled the edges of the rich lasagna.

Glancing around the table to make sure everyone was listening, she announced, "We don't eat that kind of thing where I come from."

"Oh no? What do you eat?" Stanley quickly responded. "Squirrel and possum guts?" His face was expressionless, but Arabella's was not. Her face had turned as red as her hair as she glared at Lola. "How dare you say that! Don't you know we spent hours fixing the lasagna? We made the noodles by hand. The least you can do is…is….” She burst into tears.

Ariadne put a hand on her daughter's shoulder, then rose regally from the table. She reached for the lasagna dish to carry into the kitchen. Before leaving, however, she declared, “Stanley will no longer be cooking for the entire household. Not when *some* people don't appreciate his gifts.”

Looking around the table, I saw Lola nonchalantly regarding her sharp red nails. Diego drummed his fingers on the tablecloth. He hated conflict, and it was clear to everyone that war had just been declared.

Arabella stood up, too. Wiping away her tears, she flounced into the kitchen behind her mother. Stanley slumped a little in his chair. Cooking was his passion, and he loved to feed others. Now he'd be feeding fewer people.

“I loved every bite,” I said meekly, hoping to make him feel better. “Please make it again soon.” The corners of his mouth turned up slightly. “Thank you, Beatrice. You're very kind.”

I wanted to say, “I'm not being kind, you know it's good.” But I hated to pick sides so early in the battle. At the end of the table, Lola was nibbling on the tip of her little finger. She knew she'd gone too far, but she'd never admit it. Diego couldn't bear sitting there another second. He stood up abruptly. “It's back to the studio for us, Lola. I want to work a few more hours.” Poor bloke. Because of Lola, he was back to eating from his big pot of beans again.

As for me, I didn't relish the role of peacemaker, but it didn't seem I had a choice.

CHAPTER EIGHTEEN

On Monday, time seemed to crawl by. I couldn't wait to pick up our posters at the printer's shop. As the final bell rang, Arabella begged to come with us. "I know just where to hang them," she insisted. And it was true, Arabella did know the town far better than I did. Still, Francis viewed Arabella suspiciously and only reluctantly agreed for her to come along.

And as we walked, he seemed anxious and even downhearted. I was surprised, because I figured he'd be excited to see the posters of his work. Finally, I stopped and turned to him, "What is it, Francis? Has something bad happened?" I feared he had gotten news about his father's ship. News from anywhere in the Pacific was rarely good these days. The Japanese had bombed and sunk many American vessels.

He shook his head, then glanced at Arabella and back at me. "Look, I need to tell you something. And I don't want her to hear."

Arabella didn't speak, but her lower lip trembled. She was

much more sensitive than she seemed. "Tell us both," I declared. "Arabella won't tell, will you?" I gazed forcefully at her and she shook her head. "I won't, I won't," she promised. "I won't tell a soul. Not even my mother."

I turned back to Francis.

He still hesitated, clearly worried. Finally he took a deep breath. "Okay." Then he looked around the Plaza to be sure no one could overhear. It was a sunny day, so a number of people were scattered here and there, but none were near us. "I just learned that the Japanese are coming tonight."

"The Japs? Here? Tonight?" Arabella's eyes were big as saucers.

Francis cringed hearing the word "Japs". It was usually used in a nasty way. Yet he nodded and repeated, "Tonight."

"They've been building a camp for them on the edge of town," I explained to Arabella. She was much paler than usual and her eyes remained huge.

She turned from one of us to the other. "How do you know all this?"

"My uncle told me," said Francis. "They're coming on a train about 11 p.m. Hundreds of men, just men. They're going to put them in trucks and drive them to the camp."

I had never seen Arabella speechless. I was shocked myself. And I had a question. "Why at night? And why is it a secret?"

Francis glanced around again. "I don't know. They just told my uncle and the others what was going to happen – they didn't explain why." Then he lowered his voice and added, "But I don't care. I'm going to go see the men who come tonight. Before they get locked up."

Arabella turned pale. "What? You're going to do what?"

"I'm going to hide near the train tracks 'til they arrive. Then I'm going to watch."

"But why, Francis? Why do that?" I asked.

He shrugged. "Like I said, there were Japanese living near me in San Diego. Maybe one of them is coming here."

I stared at him. "You mean…you might see…someone you know?"

He hesitated a second and then nodded. "It's possible." He shrugged. "I may know someone."

"Then I want to go, too," I said suddenly.

Arabella turned to me, aghast. "Have you gone *loco*? Why would you want to do that?"

I shook my head. "I don't know, Arabella. Honestly. I just want to be there. I want to see." I turned to Francis. "Can I? Can I go with you?"

He considered a long moment. "It's not a good idea. What if people in Santa Fe find out? What if they attack? We might get in trouble. Big trouble."

I gulped. It did sound scary. I'd never been in trouble, any kind of trouble. My heart pounded and I spoke more resolutely than I felt. "I still want to go. If you don't mind getting in trouble, why should I?"

Francis shrugged. "Okay."

So that's how the afternoon began. It was nearly 3:30 when we picked up the posters. They looked great. Francis pretended to be critical of the design. But he was beaming. As we hung up the posters, Arabella proved to be a tremendous help. She clearly wanted to show how competent she could be. She told us where to display them: the public library, the post office, city hall, the fire station, and several store windows.

Everywhere, people were eager to help with the war effort in any way they could. Finally, we had hung all of them and were ready to head home.

On our way, we passed a young boy and his mother eyeing a poster we'd hung a little while earlier. The boy was teary-eyed as he looked as his mother. "Do we have to give up Barney?" he asked. "He might be a good soldier 'cause he's got big teeth and barks loud. But he's also my best friend." The boy seemed desolate. "And what if he doesn't come home. Not ever."

His mother patted his hand. "We'll see, Billy. We all have to do our part. But I've already given the army my husband and my brother. I think that's enough for now."

They turned to leave. Billy was nearly skipping with relief. "We'll do other good stuff. We'll collect tin cans and plant a garden," he declared. "Barney would hate to leave us anyway. He'd probably run away from the army and come back home."

We watched the two leave together. Francis was the first to speak. "Gosh, it's really gonna be hard for folks."

"You wouldn't want to give up Champ, would you?" I asked.

Francis turned to me, exasperated. "Champ? You think the army would want a skinny little mongrel like him?" He shook his head. "They'll want big, strong purebred dogs, I bet."

Arabella nodded. "He's probably right. I'm glad we only have cats. I don't think you could ever train a cat for the army."

I didn't respond. I was thinking how much people were giving up for the war—their sons and brothers and husbands and fathers. And now their pets, too. It was a wrenching experience to lose a loved one, no matter whether he walked on two legs or four. I tried to change the subject. "At least we've done a good job for now." I glanced at Francis and added, "And tonight's a big night."

"You haven't changed your mind? You're sure?" His eyes were level with mine.

I returned his gaze. "Of course not. Why should I?" I wanted to sound positive. But my insides were uneasy. "I'll meet you at your house about 9:30 tonight. You think that will be enough time?"

"Plenty." He quickly turned and headed in the opposite direction.

"Gosh, Beatrice, I think you're crazy," said Arabella as we walked slowly back to her house. "You wouldn't see me within a hundred miles of that place."

Rather than appear doubtful, I responded sharply. "Maybe I am crazy, but don't you want to know what's going on in your own hometown? Why are they making it so secret?"

"I bet they have their reasons. What do you know about these Japanese men who are coming?"

The truth was that I knew absolutely nothing. I had never met a Japanese person face-to-face. It was possible they might be as horrid as the murderous Nazis. If so, they did need to be locked up.

But I had learned a lot since leaving England. Along the way, I met so many different people. First I shared my ship stateroom with three sad little Jewish children fleeing Europe. Indignant at first about sharing my room, I soon began to admire their courage. Then I made the acquaintance of Hamilton, the Negro porter, who cared for me during my long train trip. What a kind gentleman. And when I finally arrived in New Mexico, I got to know many generous, hard-working

Spanish and Indian people. All were people I'd never have met if I hadn't made this long journey. But my life was so much richer because I had met them.

And I believed it was very difficult to imagine what people are like if you haven't met them. Often, it seemed—the information you receive can give you entirely the wrong impression. It's essential, however, to learn as much as you can and to decide for yourself. Though that's not always easy, it's worth the effort.

"I know hardly anything about any Japanese at present," I admitted to Arabella. "That's why I'm going—I want to see for myself." My answer pleased me. And I thought Clem would understand, also. Although I'm afraid she would have agreed with Arabella that this late-night excursion was a very bad idea.

CHAPTER NINETEEN

That night I drank about a bucket of tea to stay awake. Arabella was awfully good about keeping her mouth shut. Several times, I could see her almost spill the beans to her mother or Stanley. But she resisted. The two of us went to our room early, on the pretext of studying for an English exam. But neither of us studied.

Arabella immersed herself in reading a new Agatha Christie murder mystery. Arabella loved mystery stories, especially those by Mrs. Christie. I mulled over a short letter I'd recently received from Clem.

March 14, 1942

Dearest Bea—

Just a quick note to let you know how I'm doing. Have finally found a place to squat here in Washington. It's just a one-bedroom apartment, and so I'm camped out in the dining room on a cot with my stuff still in my suitcase. Two young women have twin beds in the bedroom. These gals are so clever, they work at Arlington Hall, decoding German and Japanese messages. Since the work is very hush-hush, they can't even mention it in the apartment. If you come to visit (which I hope you can some day) you'll meet them— Virginia Rogers comes from rural Texas and Ruth Grace from a tiny town in Tennessee. Just goes to show there are brainy women everywhere!

Hope things are going smoothly for you. And that you're still enjoying Arabella and her family.
Much love,
Clem

I studied the letter and sighed – how lovely to visit Washington. My happy thoughts were soon interrupted, however, by loud voices. Arabella looked up, too. A squabble had clearly broken out in the living room. Ariadne and Lola were shouting at one another. The voices grew louder and louder. Then a door slammed. And it was suddenly very quiet. "Oh dear, what happened?" I murmured.

"I better find out," Arabella whispered. Then she slipped out of the room in her pajamas. When she returned a short time later, her face was pale and her hands trembled. "Oh God, oh God…this is terrible." Tears rolled down her cheeks.

"What is it? What happened?" I asked, reaching for her hand.

Arabella could barely respond. "M-my m-mother got out a knife from the kitchen, one of Stanley's sharpest carving knives, and chased Lola out the front door."

I sqeezed her hand, barely able to speak. "Why? What

happened?"

"It's gonna sound really silly," said Arabella. "But…but it was the meatballs, Stanley's meatballs." Then she explained: For dinner that night, Stanley had served a huge dish of spaghetti and meatballs. He was used to cooking for a crowd, and it was difficult for him to cut back on ingredients. Since Ariadne's declaration, however, only the four of us ate together. And this evening, my appetite had been off, due to my late-night plans. So there had been plenty of leftovers.

Later, in the kitchen when Lola and Diego came in from the studio, Stanley couldn't resist offering them some spaghetti. But, according to Arabella, Lola had tasted one and then said the meatballs smelled funny. She suggested feeding them to the cats.

I gasped. How horrid! I could imagine the effect—indeed it was like putting a lit match to dry kindling. Ariadne exploded in anger. In minutes, a major fight had developed. She and Lola started yelling about how much they hated one another.

"It got worse and worse," said Arabella, "until Mom went and got the knife." She fell back on her bed, sniffling loudly. "Oh God, what's going to happen now?"

Arabella rarely called Ariadne "Mom"—only when things were very good or very bad. I sat next to my dear friend on her bed as she wept. She was so miserable, I almost decided to cancel my plans. But her emotions must have worn her out. By 9:30, she was curled up, fast asleep.

The tea had served its purpose. I was wide awake. I hastily put on some warm trousers, a sweater, and heavy coat, and then looked around the room. Was there anything I needed? I spied my little red notebook. When I first arrived, I had often taken notes in it of things to tell my family back home. Nowadays I usually forgot to write down anything. But tonight something momentous might occur. Something I'd want to remember. So I dropped the notebook in my coat pocket. I also reached for the pair of binoculars that Clem had given me for Christmas. They were meant for birdwatching, but I figured they might be useful. Then I crept out of the house.

I had rarely been out that late. And certainly not by myself. But I knew the neighborhood well, and it was easy to find my way to the Plaza. Only a few overhead lamps lit the streets, and things looked strange in the dim light. I jogged across the empty Plaza. Something scuttled near my feet—a rat? I kept going in the direction of Griffin Street, getting somewhat lost once or twice. Being such an old city, Santa Fe is not laid out in straight lines. The streets wiggle around. But finally I reached 142 Griffin Street.

The house was nearly dark. Had Francis gone already? I glanced at my wristwatch. It was twenty minutes past ten o'clock. Much later than I had imagined. Perhaps he had assumed I wasn't coming. At that moment, however, the door cracked open and a thin form emerged.

I called softly. When he came over, I apologized for being late. Though I didn't describe the major battle at Arabella's house. I knew Arabella wouldn't want anyone to know.

"I figured you'd come." He glanced at the binoculars hanging around my neck. "Glad you got those." Then he and I quickly headed toward the train station. It was only a few blocks. But these streets were even darker than downtown. Still, a few people were out. From their loud, raucous voices, I guessed they had come from nearby saloons or bars. We

116

avoided being seen by staying in the shadows and making as little noise as possible.

Finally we reached the train station. Francis stopped and peered around. "That's my uncle over there," he whispered, pointing to six or seven men. "Those are all guards, like him. They must be waiting here for the train."

I stared into the dark. I could barely make out the figures of the men, about twenty yards away, but I could see the lit ends of a half dozen cigarettes. The glow revealed where they were standing. Then the wind shifted, and I could hear their voices, as well.

"I think we're safe here," I said, flattening myself against a wall. "Let's stay."

He nodded. We were both silent a few moments. From across the tracks, we heard the guards laughing loudly. Francis turned to me, his face tense. "My uncle is my dad's older brother, but not like my dad at all. He never wanted me here. Now he puts me to work, doing chores. 'You gotta earn yer keep,' he says." Francis buttoned his mouth and turned back around to continue watching for the train.

After a moment, he whispered, "You probably wonder why I wanted to come tonight. Why it was so important." Before I could answer, he responded, "I'm looking for *one* man. Mr. Michimo Haiyoko."

I was stunned. He was going to so much trouble to see one man who *might* be on this train. "Who is he?" I asked.

He hesitated a second, his thoughts clearly returning to happier times. "Mr. Haiyoko had a flower shop near our house," he finally said. "I used to pass it every day on my way to school." Francis gave me a sideways look, before adding, "I like flowers."

He didn't need to explain further. Thirteen-year-old boys weren't supposed to like flowers.

"Sometimes I'd stop and look and smell the beautiful bunches of lilies or roses. If the store wasn't busy, Mr. Haiyoko would come out and talk to me. Tell me about the different flowers, their names, where they grew." Even in the dark, I could see a tiny smile on his lips. "One day, he asked if I wanted to see his paintings of flowers. It was the first time I'd seen real pictures that weren't in a book." Francis paused, as if remembering that special moment. "As soon as I saw them, I wanted to paint pictures, too. So Mr. Haiyoko gave me a thick pencil with a soft lead—the kind you draw with. He said artists always start out drawing first." He glanced at me. "So that's how I started."

Now I understood completely. I understood why it was so important to Francis to learn if Mr. Haiyoko was on this train. Sometimes someone offers you a gift. It can be something as small as a pencil, but it points you in a different direction. It gives you a new way to think about everything.

I turned to Francis, "Why do you think he's on *this* train? There are a lot of other camps for Japanese people around the country. He could be anywhere."

Francis nodded. "Yeah, I know. But my uncle says there are only going to be men in this camp. And the men were chosen because they're not farmers or workers." He gazed at me. "They're teachers and ministers, and store owners like Mr. Haiyoko. You see people in San Diego liked him. He had a successful business." He seemed eager to convince me. "That's why I think they may have picked him, too."

Francis turned back to stare at the bare tracks ahead. I stamped my feet to keep warm. The temperature was dropping.

Suddenly I spied another figure, some distance away. There was someone else lurking around in the dim light, trying not to be seen. I raised the binoculars to see better, and then gasped, "Oh my gosh, it's him!"

Francis put his finger to his lips, cautioning me. "Who?"

"Th-the Swiss man," I stammered.

"How do you know?"

"He limps."

"Other people limp."

"No, it's him. I'm certain of it." My stomach had been fluttery with excitement; now I felt almost sick with fear. Why was Mr. Prestre here? Why would he want to see the Japanese people arrive? Did he know I was here, too? He didn't seem to have seen us, and I desperately hoped he wouldn't.

Suddenly I didn't want to stay any longer. Francis had a reason to be there, but I didn't. I turned to go.

Then the guards shouted something. And we could hear the train rumbling on the tracks, heading this way. I forgot about leaving as Francis and I leaned forward, watching intently. We saw the train roll into the station, a short distance away. It stopped with a loud squealing lurch. The prison guards sprang into action, moving toward the train doors. Most of them carried rifles.

"See my uncle," Francis murmured, pointing at a large, bearded man in a cap with flaps that covered his ears. He was less than twenty feet away. The guards pulled open the doors, ordering the people off the train. The Japanese men climbed off, one by one, looking hesitant, confused. Their hands were fastened behind their backs, like criminals. Even though their faces revealed little emotion, I could sense their shock, uncertainty and anxiety. Yet they tried to obey orders with dignity. The guards were mostly helpful, speaking gently and carefully guiding them. Only a few were rough, jostling the men and urging them to move more quickly.

I glanced around for the Swiss man. Was he still there? I didn't see him.

Then Francis poked me and began pointing. "That's him, Mr. Haiyoko!" he whispered, his face tight with excitement. "You see him? He's elderly and walking slowly."

I nodded, though in the dim light, most of the men looked similar to me.

But Francis was certain. "I knew he'd come," he said softly. "I knew it."

Because he was slow, one of the guards—it might have been Francis's uncle—nudged Mr. Haiyoko forward with the butt of his rifle. Francis was furious. "Damn him," he hissed. "Can't he see he's doing his best?"

That's when the notion first crossed my mind—how strange this was. Why were these men being locked up in a camp? They looked quite ordinary, not a bit dangerous. How could anyone be afraid of an old man like Mr. Haiyoko? A flower salesman? I couldn't quite grasp it all in my mind. I could only guess that in wartime, people behave in odd ways that they normally wouldn't.

The Japanese were quickly loaded onto trucks. Then the trucks took off, one by one, down the dark road. Suddenly I felt totally exhausted. "Let's go, Francis. At least you know he's here."

Francis moved slowly, his mind still on Mr. Haiyoko. "I've got to speak to him. I've gotta get in the camp and speak to him."

"How can you do that?" I whispered. "Would your uncle help?"

"My uncle?" He snapped. "I'd never tell my uncle."

Finally, we headed back toward his house. Francis remained deep in thought, and I was silent, as well. Saying goodbye at his house, he muttered, "There must be a way."

I kept going, walking as fast as possible and even jogging a bit. Reaching the Plaza, I remembered the red notebook in my pocket. Too much had been happening for me to take notes, but I would write everything down later tonight. I didn't want to forget anything I'd seen.

The sight of the "Swiss" man, Mr. Prestre, had been especially jarring. Why had he been there? What was he looking for? And had he seen me? Was he even now *tracking* me? What a horrid, horrid thought.

I didn't dare glance around to see. Without intending to, I found myself running, fast as possible, through the dark, empty streets.

CHAPTER TWENTY

I slept through the morning. When I awoke, sunshine was streaming in our bedroom. Lazily turning over and stretching, I glimpsed Arabella. She sat on her bed, slumped, her cheeks red and wet with tears.

"What's wrong, Arabella?"

"It's awful, awful." She could hardly speak through her tears. "When Lola came back, she and mother yelled at each other. They screamed so loud, a neighbor called the police."

"The police?" I gasped.

She nodded. "Mother has decided she can't stay here anymore. She can't live in the same house as Lola."

"So she's going to look for another house?"

Arabella looked stricken. She could barely utter the next words. "She isn't...she isn't going to look for another house here." Arabella shook her head. "They're leaving town. She says her talent and spirit are too big for a little town like Santa Fe. They're going to Cleveland. Stanley knows people there.

And they have an opera company there."

Now it was my turn to worry. If they left town, what would Arabella do? If she left with them, what would I do? Would I be homeless?

Arabella must have guessed what I was thinking. She slumped further down on the bed. "Don't worry. I'm not going," she said in a lifeless voice. "Mother says she doesn't know what's ahead. She has no idea where they'll be staying." Her face was clouded with disappointment. "They're leaving the day after tomorrow, as soon as they can pack up the Buick. Ariadne just drove to the service station to see if the tires are in good enough shape."

She fell back on the bed, staring upward. "I...I think she's glad to have an excuse to go."

"Oh no, Arabella, I'm certain you're wrong about that." I climbed out of my bed to sit next to her on hers. She lay limp, like a corpse.

Her mother had barely been in town a month. For Arabella, the month had been pure heaven. It seemed unbelievably cruel that Ariadne was leaving again so soon. Leaving her daughter behind.

Arabella sounded resigned. "I'll stay here with Uncle Diego and Lola. It will be just like before. And, of course, you can stay with us." She rolled over. "Please, please, Beatrice, say that you'll stay with us. I just...I just...really need someone here."

Her voice broke and tears flowed again. She grabbed a pillow, hugging it tight and soaking the pillowcase with her tears. Indeed, it was impossible to imagine deserting Arabella now. She was already so unhappy. Even if Clem found out what happened as she was bound to, sooner or later, I doubted that she'd insist that I relocate. She'd always had doubts about the stability of the household. And she'd been proven correct. But, at present, I had little choice. I could explain that to her. I needed to stay here and take care of my friend.

These thoughts were interrupted by a knock on the door. "May I come in?" Stanley's voice was gentle as he cracked open the door.

"Sorry, but perhaps that's not a good idea." I jerked my head toward Arabella on the bed. "She's extremely unhappy."

He nodded. "I just wanted to say we're…well, I'm going to fix a really great meal." He looked sad. "One of our last, I'm afraid, before we take off."

I thanked him and closed the door. My stomach began to rumble at the very idea of a meal. But I had a feeling that Arabella would not relish anything, no matter how delicious. It turned out I was wrong, however—food possesses a magical power to transform emotions. Only a few moments later, a teary voice emerged from the red-haired bundle on the bed.

"Did Stanley say what he was fixing?" Arabella murmured. "I wonder what it could be? We don't have much in the icebox."

I smiled, glad that Arabella's mood was shifting. "I have no idea," I replied, "but if Stanley's cooking, I'm sure it will be magnificent."

"You think I should offer to help?" she asked plaintively. "He's always appreciated my help."

"That's a splendid idea!" I exclaimed. "I'm sure he'd appreciate any assistance, but especially yours." An untidy mess, Arabella crawled out of bed and went to rinse her face with cold water from the washbasin.

As soon as she left, I began thinking again of my own predicament. Indeed I would have to remain, at least for a while. And I had no doubt that Clem would understand. I could honestly tell her that I had gotten accustomed to living in disorder. Or rather, I had learned how to maintain my own sense of order in the midst of others' disorder. Which she probably would agree is a very good skill to have. In the future, once Arabella seemed steady enough, then perhaps I could make a change. Though, at the moment, I had no clue when that would be or where I'd go. In fact, I really didn't want to think about it. Make another big change? I dreaded the thought.

The next few days were grueling. Lola believed she had been victorious in the struggle between the two women. After all, Ariadne had been forced out, while she was remaining. Her nose had always been a bit turned up, but now it was sky high. Arabella so despised her that I feared she might grab a kitchen knife and plunge it into Lola's long, white neck. Finally, even Uncle Diego was fed up with the southern belle. He banished her to the studio, full time.

After her weeks of ecstasy, Arabella was now plunged into sorrow. Meanwhile, Ariadne rallied every ounce of maternal affection she possessed and poured it on her daughter. Whenever I entered the living room, the two were draped around each other. "You'll come live with us in Cleveland," her mother declared again and again. "As soon as we're settled, I'll send you a train ticket."

From Arabella's expression, however, I guessed she had heard similar promises in the past. She knew she should just hold tightly to her mother for now. Once Ariadne was gone, she was truly gone. At least, until she miraculously reappeared—no one knew when.

Stanley also was very kind. He asked Arabella which were her favorite dishes. Then he wrote down the recipes in a large notebook. The two sat side by side on the big, overstuffed sofa and read them aloud together. "You'll have no trouble making this one," Stanley would say. "Just simmer a pork chop in the bottom of the pan before adding the tomato sauce. Got it?" She'd nod obediently while he continued to make suggestions. "Simmer the onion until it's golden, but be careful and don't burn the edges, understand?"

Obviously, these dreams of future meals comforted Arabella. Yet I questioned whether she'd actually make them on her own. I figured soon we would all be eating from Uncle Diego's pot of beans.

At last, goodbyes had to be said. The Buick was all packed. Stanley fumbled with a road map, hoping to make it to Oklahoma by nightfall. Arabella was stoically calm, her tears mostly spent. She mustered a sort of fake smile when kissing Ariadne for the final time. Then she handed her mother a tin of thick, chewy brownies she'd secretly prepared for their trip. Stanley and her mother expressed huge delight, of course. And there was another round of hugs.

Naturally, Lola was not present. Uncle Diego kissed his sister on the cheek sadly and muttered, "I'll take good care of your daughter." Then he shook hands with Stanley and fled back to his paints and easel.

Ariadne saved her last farewell for me. "You are a beautiful, brave girl and the best friend Arabella ever had." She kissed me. "Sometimes it's possible for a few good things to come out of terrible things like wars." I stared back at her. I hated what she'd just said, but it was undeniably true. Settling into her car seat, Ariadne blew a few more kisses to her daughter and then they were gone.

A freezing rain had begun to fall by the time the Buick pulled away. Somehow the wet, gray day reminded me of London, eighteen months before, when I had left my family. The lump in my throat loomed large and solid, just as it had then.

"Oh, Arabella!" I grabbed her hand and squeezed, knowing the anguish she must be feeling.

But her pale face was frozen, a smile fixed on her lips. "I kept half the brownies," she murmured. "They're still warm. Let's go eat some."

And that's what we did, we ate every one.

CHAPTER TWENTY-ONE

Francis had never been talkative. But for over a week, he was silent as the grave. I tried several times to speak to him. I wanted to know if he had succeeded in contacting Mr. Haiyoko. Every time I asked, however, he turned away abruptly and ignored my question. Then he stared out the window or gazed down at a textbook on his desk. I guessed he wasn't actually seeing what was outside or in the book.

Finally, I decided to take a different tack. I'd speak to him about the Dogs for Defense poster. I called to him as he hurriedly left after school. When he paused, I ran up. "The poster—our poster—has truly worked."

"What?" He looked surprised, as if he'd forgotten that project completely.

"Mr. Scott has received dozens of calls from people wishing to contribute their dogs," I exclaimed. "He's arranging for a public meeting this Saturday. He's asking for people to bring the dogs to the Santa Fe High School playing field near the

Plaza. He and Mr. Tremble, the vet, will examine each one and decide which to take. Why don't you come, too?"

Francis considered and then shrugged. "Maybe. On Saturdays I have to mop all the floors." He turned to go. I watched his thin, slightly hunched back as he headed down the street. Poor Francis, hardly anything seemed to please him.

I walked in the direction of Arabella's house. I had barely gone halfway when Esteban caught up and fell in beside me. What a lovely suprise. For a moment, it felt like old times. He'd grown a bit taller, but otherwise looked the same—a lock of black hair still fell in his face and a sly smile danced on his lips. Then suddenly his expression changed to a scowl and his tone sounded suspicious. "You and that new guy are good friends, eh?"

For a moment I had no idea whom he was talking about. Then suddenly I knew, and had to suppress a giggle.

"You don't mean Francis, do you?"

Esteban nodded grimly, his gaze shifting away from me.

"We talk about Dogs for Defense," I explained. "He drew the poster." I tried to engage Esteban's attention. "It's our effort to help the win the war."

He considered a second. "That why you two are together so much?"

"Yes." I slowed my step and turned to face him. Seeing him here, so close, made me realize how much I had missed him. I wanted to tell him, but felt unsure how.

He glanced back at me, also fumbling for words. "People, people are saying—they say he's your boyfriend."

"Oh no," I quickly protested. "He's not my boyfriend. He couldn't be my boyfriend. Because, because…"

I breathlessly halted on the verge of saying, "Because *you're* my boyfriend."

But the words stuck in my mouth. Having never had a boyfriend, how could I know precisely what one was? Just because we had spent an entire day together last summer riding ponies at his grandfather's pueblo; just because we had cooled our sweaty skins by jumping in the Rio Grande; just because we'd held hands as we struggled against the pull of the river's strong current—that didn't really make us boyfriend-girlfriend, did it?

His dark eyes fastened on mine. Perhaps he was remembering those same precious moments. He might even recall the tingle as our hands touched beneath the cold swift water. His eyes lost focus as he leaned in closer. And closer. Was he…was he going to kiss me?

A live current ran straight through me. Deep inside I felt a thrilling warmth. A second or two passed like this as he seemed to draw near and nearer…but our lips never met. Abruptly Esteban stepped back, his gaze shifted. Though the warm sensation within me lingered….

"I never thought that guy was your boyfriend," he muttered. "It's just you spend so much time with him."

"Well, we're trying to help the war effort," I repeated and added eagerly, "I'd really love your help." I could feel my face redden. "I mean *we'd* love your help—Arabella and Francis and I.

Esteban shruggged. "Maybe, sometime." His lopsided grin kicked in. "How 'bout living with Arabella? Heard there was some fireworks over there?" His smile grew wider. This was the Esteban, my pal, always ready to make a joke, tease, fool around. We resumed walking again.

"Oh dear, it's been horrible!" I exclaimed. "Arabella's mother and Stanley have left. Arabella is worse than I've ever seen her. She mopes all day. And at night I hear her sobbing. Some mornings she won't even get up for school."

He shook his head sympathetically. "*Pobre chica.*" No one in town liked to see Arabella unhappy. She was usually such a cheerful, upbeat person with friends everywhere. "Her mother won't come back, eh?

"Not as long as Lola's here. They hate each other." We had reached Arabella's house, so I stopped. "I so miss your mother's food," I exclaimed. "Stanley fixed a lot of delicious things but nothing like her enchiladas or posole."

He reached over and gave my arm a friendly pinch. "Nobody said you couldn't come visit. We aren't on the other side of the moon. Visit us, anytime!"

I knew Esteban would take off in a second. He had gone out of his way to walk this far with me. So I spoke quickly. "What about your cousins? Do you know anything?"

His smile disappeared and his eyes narrowed. "We heard they all had to retreat into the jungle. The whole battalion." He frowned. "The U.S. commander told 'em to. And now they're in a really bad way—not enough food or ammunition. And still getting the heck bombed out of 'em." He turned to go, then glanced back. "Those damn Japs. They brung a bunch of 'em here. Did you know that? Lucky for them, they're behind barbed wire and a high fence, 'cause there are people here who'd like to knock 'em up good," he muttered. "Then they'd be sorry, really sorry, for what they've done."

His final look was dark and menacing as he took off down

the street. I wished I had a chance to speak with him more. Yet I understood his anger. It's horrible to know that people you love are in danger. And if you feel helpless to protect them, it's easy to become hostile. I felt the same way in London when I saw homes and shops and churches destroyed. Or when I learned of a teacher or a shopkeeper or a child killed.

It might not be fair for people in Santa Fe to vent their resentment against the men in the camp. But what did they know? They didn't know any Japanese personally—they only knew what they read in the newspaper or heard on the radio. Naturally they were fearful and angry.

Then I remembered the men I'd seen climb off the train—their sad faces and hunched shoulders. How they had attempted to remain dignified despite their worry and fears. They weren't soldiers. They had been shopkeepers and teachers and preachers, like people here.

If I had spoken to Esteban, would it have mattered? His feelings were so strong, at present, I doubt he would have heard anything I said.

CHAPTER TWENTY-TWO

I wondered whether to tell Francis what Esteban had told me. It would worry him, no doubt, to imagine the threat to the camp. And what could he do? In any case, Francis didn't give me the chance to say anything. The next day, he rushed up before the first bell rang. "I'm going inside the camp this afternoon," he announced happily.

"Oh my goodness," I responded. "How did you manage that?"

"The Japanese have been asking for cigarettes, gum, and stuff like that. They've got the money to pay for it. But someone has to go to the Cash and Carry Store and buy it." Francis grinned. "My uncle wants to make some extra money. He says he can buy the stuff and charge a little extra for it. But he doesn't have the time. So I volunteered."

"Will they actually let you go inside?"

"I think so," he replied. "If I do all the work and my uncle makes the money, he'll see that I get in."

"So you'll get to see Mr. Haiyoko."

Francis nodded, still beaming. "I sure hope so."

All day I watched as Francis fidgeted at his desk. He glanced at the clock every ten minutes. When the final bell rang, he leapt out of his seat and ran for the door.

Arabella was finally back at school most of the time. I had hoped seeing her friends (and especially seeing Hank) would cheer her up. It did a little, at least for the duration of the day. And she seemed in a remarkably good mood as we walked home together. She spoke a bit about this and that, as usual, then she said, "I wonder if it's hard to buy poison."

"Poison?" I asked blithely, my mind still on Francis's news. "It might be difficult to purchase. Do you need any?"

Her response was equally cheerful. "Yes, I'm planning to kill someone."

I didn't need to ask whom she wanted to kill, but my mood was no longer light-hearted. "You wouldn't really, would you?"

"Beatrice!" She whipped around. "Just imagine, *your* uncle's girlfriend driving *your* mother out of town." Then she began sniffling. "My darling mother—she'll probably never return."

I had imagined Arabella had already cried herself dry, but apparently not. Tears seeped out of her eyes. She wiped her runny nose with the sleeve of her sweater. She was clearly still miserable. Her mood had gone from dizzily high to abysmally low in a matter of seconds. I hated to see her suffer so without being able to do or say anything.

Why hadn't her mother tried a bit harder to stay in town? She had allowed a few quarrels with Lola to dislodge her. Maybe she had been looking for an excuse to leave. But I could hardly say that to Arabella. Not in the murderous mood she was in at present.

"What about rat poison? Isn't that easy to get?" she continued. "I wonder if I should write Agatha Christie. She knows a lot about poison. She almost always uses it as the murder weapon."

"Well, I'm sure she knows a lot more about poison than you. But if you write to her with the intention of using it to kill someone, then I doubt you'll receive a nice reply." I was worried. Arabella looked far more resolute than usual. It seemed unlikely that my sweet, lively friend could ever kill someone, even with such a strong motive. Yet I knew some people did crazy things on the spur of the moment. They behaved in ways they regretted their entire lives. Arabella was so upset at present, she might do something extremely foolish. "You must stop thinking this way at once," I admonished my friend. "It's…it's not healthy."

Arabella shrugged and said no more about it. From her expression, though, I thought she might still be contemplating Lola's murder. I knew, however, that she rarely held onto any idea for very long. So I decided to simply change the subject. I struggled to think of something that would totally grab her attention. Finally, I burst out, "I just learned that Francis has a Japanese friend. He's one of the prisoners they brought to the camp."

That definitely did the trick. Arabella turned and stared at me, her eyes big, her mouth agape. The notion of murdering Lola had clearly flown out of her head. Then she wanted to know all the details: How had Francis become friends with a Japanese man? Who was the man? Why had he come to the Santa Fe camp?

I didn't think it would hurt to tell her most everything. And it was exactly the sort of story that enchanted Arabella. "The Japanese are very artistic," she said. "My mother once played Madame Butterfly, and her kimono was magnificent."

Still, I was a bit worried about her knowing so much. Francis hadn't specified that his relationship with Mr. Haiyoko was secret, but he clearly wouldn't want everyone to know it. "Please, Arabella, don't tell anyone else," I gripped her hands to emphasize. "You understand?"

She nodded, making a gesture of zipping shut her mouth. "Lips sealed," she mumbled and glumly added, "Who could I tell anyway? Now that Ariadne's gone."

I was sorry we'd returned to that subject. How could I continue to distract her? I was searching my mind desperately when we reached the house and I spied the postal box—that gave me an idea. I led Arabella toward the kitchen, chattering away. "I recently received a very odd cake recipe from Mother. In England, they've had to be extremely creative to cope with the shortages of butter and sugar and flour. You can't guess what goes in it!"

When Arabella learned of the secret ingredient, she was immediately game to give it a try. That's why Arabella and I spent a good part of the afternoon grating carrots into a bowl. We made the most unusual cake, quite orange-looking and a bit rough in texture, but very tasty.

Even Uncle Diego thought so. "What do you call it?" he asked.

"Carrot cake," we sang out together, giggling.

Lola watched as we gobbled up our slices. "Where's my piece?"

"Oh, I didn't think you'd want any," Arabella purred. "It's a bit fattening. And I'd hate for you to ruin your figure." She grinned like the Cheshire Cat. "Then you couldn't model for my uncle."

Lips pursed, Lola stalked off. She loved sweet things. But she knew she couldn't say anything offensive to Uncle Diego's niece; he wouldn't allow it. I figured Lola was quite lucky if Arabella avenged herself in this manner. It was much better to miss a slice of cake than to be poisoned.

The next day at school, I was eager to discover whether Francis had made contact with Mr. Haiyoko. It was impossible to read his blank face, however. It revealed neither excitement nor disappointment. So I cornered him at lunch.

"How did you fare? Did you get a chance to speak to Mr. Haiyoko?"

He shook his head impatiently. "There's over four hundred men there. It woulda' been blind luck to see him." He fell silent for a moment. "You know what they want most? Not cigarettes or candy…they want stamps." His face was sober. "They want to write to their families—their wives, their children."

"Where are their wives and children?"

"They've been put in other camps in far-off places like Utah and Wyoming. There's one or two in southern New Mexico, also." He added, "I didn't have any stamps. So they gave me letters to mail and money for postage. I've got a whole stack."

"Where are they going?"

He shrugged. "Manzanar, Posten, Tule Lake, and Heart Mountain. I've never heard of those places, have you?"

"My goodness, so many people, so many camps!" I protested. "How strange to put women and children and even little babies in camps behind barbed wire. Does the US government really fear children and babies?"

"I dunno." Francis sighed. "I left a note for Mr. Haiyoko. I hope he gets it."

He walked away, his shoulders slumped, as usual. I hoped he did find Mr. Haiyoko. It seemed so absolutely essential to him, like the only thing in life that mattered.

CHAPTER TWENTY-THREE

The Dogs for Defense event was very festive. Arabella and I came early and put up different-colored balloons. Fortunately, it was one of the first days of April and quite fair and sunny. A number of people came by to observe, including Hank. He was curious to learn if his dog, Dinger, would be eligible. The dog was a small, black, curly-haired mutt. In fact, Dinger was one of the ugliest dogs I've ever seen. But Arabella *oohed* and *ahhed* over the beast like he was Rin Tin Tin himself. I couldn't believe Hank could take her chatter seriously. But he seemed delighted by her enthusiasm. In fact, after the dog was rejected for being too old to train, the two—or rather, the three of them—drifted off together, with Arabella now grasping Dinger's leash.

I was quite content to remain with Mr. Scott. He was very well organized, handing me a checklist to fill out for each dog. It contained ordinary questions about the dog's health and behavior.

Twenty or more dogs, all breeds and sizes, were milling around. Every sort of person had brought their pets, from youngsters to elderly men and women. I queued everyone up and handed out pencils and the questionnaires.

Miss White came briefly to oversee the operation. "People are being very brave and generous, don't you think?" she said. "It can't be easy for anyone to give up their family pet."

"Yes, ma'am, they are being very patriotic," I replied. We watched for another minute or two until she spoke again. "My sister, Martha, would have enjoyed this very much."

"Your sister?" I asked.

The sorrowful look I'd seen in her eyes returned. "Yes, Martha loved animals—dogs, horses—any animals." She glanced at me. "I'm sorry that you didn't get to know her. She died several years ago."

"I'm sorry, too," I murmured. Now I understood why Miss White seemed so lonely. She was still mourning the loss of her sister.

"Martha was the peppy, outgoing one," she added. "Always full of ideas about fun things to do—parties, plays, pageants." She sighed. "Without her adventurous spirit, I have to find my own way."

"You are finding your own way," I said quickly. And I truly believed she was – not just the Dogs for Defense but the health projects on the pueblos. She seemed very dedicated. But Miss White may not have heard me because, at that moment, Mr. Scott signaled her to come over and inspect a large Airedale. "What an excellent dog. Don't you think this is precisely the kind of animal we're looking for?" His face was all smiles. The Airedale was pulling on its leash and barking at every dog that passed. It seemed the opposite of Miss White's Irish wolfhounds, who were so calm and steadfast.

Miss White shared my doubts. "Are you sure, Alex, you can manage to train him? He seems to have some poor habits."

"Absolutely, Miss White. He's young and healthy and smart. Give me two months with this dog, and you'll see an amazing change." He petted the dog as if eager to transform this unruly pup into a first-class military dog.

"Well, you know best," concluded Miss White. Then she turned to me. "Thanks so much for promoting this event. Clem was right, you are a tremendous help. And if…." She paused to consider her words. "And if you would like to have tea with me again some day, please let me know. I'd be delighted."

Without thinking, I curtsied politely. My goodness, what a surprise. I hadn't curtsied to an elder since leaving Great Britain. Yet it seemed appropriate. She was so elegant and sophisticated and reserved, just like an English aristocrat. "Yes, Miss White, I'd be delighted, too."

As soon as she departed, I turned back to see which dog Mr. Scott was examining now. It was a great shock, if not horror, to see him engrossed in a conversation with Mr. Prestre. Mr. Prestre!

My skin suddenly felt cold and clammy; I could barely breathe. What was he doing *here*? Why had he been in the hills above the city? Or at the train station, observing the Japanese prisoners? Why did he always seem to be in the same place as I? Was he a spy? Was he trailing me?

Whatever the answers, I was eager to slip away before he could see me. Then his gaze fell on me and I froze. Yet he didn't seem to notice me at all. He remained earnestly speaking to

Mr. Scott for several moments. The two seemed to be arguing. Then, scowling, Mr. Prestre hastily left.

The obvious thing was to ask Mr. Scott what they were talking about. I moved closer to him. But he was already examining another dog, a handsome Dalmatian. He seemed quite pleased with the dog, which stood quietly and obediently as he spoke with its owner. She was a lovely, young woman with soft, curly hair. "Yes, Perdita is a great dog. My husband has a fine Dalmatian, too. In fact, we met because of our love for these dogs. Since then, we've raised several large litters."

"I hope you realize what it means to give her up to the army," said Mr. Scott. "The dog could be wounded or killed. Even worse, it might come back so stunned or mentally damaged from warfare that it won't even recognize you."

The woman's voice trembled a bit as she replied, "I do know. My brother lost his sight in the Great War. And has never been the same. But...but we do want to find a way to help." She turned to her dog. "And I believe Perdita would want to do her part, as well."

"She does seem like a smart dog and already well trained," said Mr. Scott. "I look forward to working with her." The two shook hands. "But if you change your mind in the next few days, please call and let us know."

The woman nodded and then gave her dog a final hug and handed the leash to Mr. Scott. Walking away, she pulled a lace-edged hankie from her purse and dabbed her eyes.

Somehow, her tears sparked some unhappy feelings of my own. For weeks, I had needed to be strong and positive for Arabella and for Francis and even a bit for Esteban. For everyone, it seemed, except myself. All of a sudden my face felt hot and I was fighting tears.

Mr. Scott must have noticed that I was losing my composure, for he handed me a large, white cotton handkerchief. "Ah, lass, I'm not surprised you're feeling the grief of it. I am myself," he said. "It's mighty hard. And a very big-hearted thing to give your own pet away. Especially when it's going to go to something as bloody awful as a war."

While I wiped my tears away, Mr. Scott examined several dogs. Most were rejected—too old, too young, too little, too nervous, too fat—but he found a few worthy of being in the program. By the day's end, he'd gathered a small band that included the Dalmatian and the Airedale, plus a Bloodhound, a Boxer, and a Cairn Terrier. Regarding the Cairn, he said, "Small, yes, but tough and clever and brave."

"And they come from Scotland, don't they?" I said.

"Ya got me there, lass." He grinned, "Tha' might have something to do with my decision."

By day's end, I was quite tired out and ready to head back to Arabella's. On the way home, however, I stopped short. "Drat," I said outloud. "I forgot to ask about Mr. Prestre."

CHAPTER TWENTY-FOUR

Days passed, but I couldn't rid myself of the thought of Mr. Prestre. Some instinct told me he was up to no good. But what was it? I decided to talk it over with Arabella. It would be good to keep her brain occupied, in case she was still planning to poison Lola. Besides, she might have some good advice.

"Beatrice, it's so obvious. He must be a spy—a Nazi spy!" she exclaimed as soon as she heard. "You've got to tell someone about him."

"Who would I tell?"

"The mayor or the chief of police or the governor or our principal Mrs. Belfrey—somebody!"

We were sitting at the kitchen table, each eating from a bowl of beans and munching on tortillas. It was tasty and we were hungry. The visions of Stanley's fancy dishes were fading. Even the luscious smells that had lingered in the kitchen for a while were disappearing. And Arabella hadn't opened the recipe book even once. She claimed the very idea of cooking without Stanley depressed her.

"I wish Clem were here. I could tell her. She's so sensible, she'd know exactly what to do," I replied.

"That would be best," said Arabella. "But she's not here, and she's depending on you to do the right thing."

I nodded. How well I knew. If only I knew the right thing to do. But I was still uncertain about the correct course of action.

"I can't tell anyone about going to the train station. That would be ratting on Francis, and I'm sure he'd get in big trouble. Plus, Mr. Prestre spoke to Mr. Scott right in the open. He didn't look as if he had anything to hide."

"Spies are sneaky," said Arabella. "They have things called *aliases*."

"What is that?"

"An alias is a pretend identity. It's like the part in a play or an opera. Some days you play a king and the next day you play a beggar," explained Arabella. "He could have told Mr. Scott anything. But that doesn't mean he's not a spy."

She paused, clearly thinking hard. "Have you written down every time you've seen Mr. Prestre in your red notebook?"

I nodded. "Most every time, I believe." But I wasn't sure. I had neglected my journal quite a bit of late. Too much was happening, too fast, to record every incident.

"Well, you need to write stuff down. So you can tell someone all the details—the places, the dates, everything."

I gazed at my friend. Sometimes she amazed me. It must be all the murder mysteries she read—what she was learning was definitely not in our geometry textbook.

The next morning, we were both brushing our teeth when

Arabella paused, toothbrush in hand. "You think Lola would taste rat poison in her toothpaste?" She paused to rinse out her mouth with water, then looked at me sincerely. "That would work, don't you think?"

I didn't respond. I had assumed the threat of murder was over, but I was clearly mistaken. No, this was serious and dreadful. Arabella was thinking lucidly (how simple to put poison in Lola's toothpaste)—but her idea was utterly insane. She must be stopped, and soon. I puzzled over what to do as we headed to school. How could I possibly avoid this calamity that was looming closer and closer?

Later, sitting at my desk, stewing, I hardly heard what the teacher was saying. I worried over the problem like a cat playing with a dead mouse. First I'd consider one idea, then another.

I was still baffled when Francis bounded over to my desk. From his quick step, I guessed that he'd made contact with Mr. Haiyoko. Indeed, he said, the two of them had spent forty minutes talking together yesterday afternoon. Mr. Haiyoko had almost been in tears upon seeing him. He told Francis that he now felt much less alone, even without his precious flowers.

"I wish you knew how good Mr. Haiyoko is to me," said Francis shyly. "He's like a grandfather, the best grandfather a kid could have. So kind and gentle."

His eyes shone. "And he wants to see my pictures. I can't wait to show him what I've been doing."

"That sounds lovely, Francis. Really, it does." I was sincerely pleased for his sake. "Is he comfortable in the camp?"

"It's okay. Very simple, very plain. There are only tents

now, but they're planning to build barracks. It's dull. No color, no music, no flowers." His face turned grave. "But the men get plenty to eat, and Mr. Haiyoko says most of the guards are considerate. Plus, next summer the men hope to plant their own garden with vegetables and flowers." He shook his head. "Still, I think it's totally unfair. Imagine being snatched away from your home and family."

"That's not hard for me to imagine," I replied, quickly bristling. "Because that's what happened to me. I was forced to leave the home and family I loved." All of a sudden, I felt grumpy and defensive. "Lots of people all over the world have lost their homes and families because of this war. And just remember, *we* didn't start it. The Japanese should have thought of all the bad things that could happen before bombing us."

Francis glared at me. "No, we didn't start it and neither did the people in the camps – don't forget, Bea, even if they were born in Japan, they live in this country now. Most are American citizens." He looked disgusted. "You sound like Donald Riggsbee."

That shut me up. He was right, of course. How could I have become so muddled? I was behaving just like Donald who lumped all Japanese together into sneaky, cruel, war-loving people. Or like Esteban, filled with rage. After Pearl Harbor, I knew many Americans agreed with them. But wasn't that precisely the sort of wickedness being carried out by the Nazis? They were separating people by race and ethnic group, exalting one group and condemning another. That's how they justified murdering the Jewish people and many others. And that was a major reason why the Brits and the Americans were fighting *against* the Nazis—at least that's what my father had told me. Before I came to the United States, he had stated clearly: "I wouldn't want any child of mine to grow up under the cruel regime that rules Nazi Germany at present." So how could *we* behave in a similar manner? Honestly, it was so confusing! Utterly topsy-turvy. No, that was too frivolous a word, too silly. And what was happening now was serious and sad and scary. I didn't know the right word for it. Maybe I'd know when I was older. Yet I hoped that what was happening now wouldn't be happening then. I hoped the world would be at peace in the future. Was that too much to hope for?

Francis, however, didn't stay angry. "Mr. Haiyoko did tell me the men here think they're lucky that the camp is located in such a beautiful place," he said. "They call Santa Fe *San Te He*, "Land of Many Mountains."" Returning to his desk, he sat down. His back seemed straighter than usual and his chin a little higher. I guessed he was already looking forward to his next visit with Mr. Haiyoko. I was glad I hadn't shared what I'd heard earlier from Esteban. It would have ruined his day.

CHAPTER TWENTY-FIVE

Any concern for Francis and the Japanese camp had to be postponed, however. For I was trying to tackle a very worrisome and much-closer-to-home problem. Finally, however, a plan had emerged in my brain.

Evading Arabella, I skipped lunch and went directly to the principal's office. Fortunately, Mrs. Belfrey, the principal, was eating lunch at her desk. "Is it possible to place a long-distance telephone call?" I asked. Mrs. Belfrey looked surprised. "Is there an emergency? Do you want to call Miss Pope?"

I shook my head. "It is an emergency, I believe. But I don't need to call Clem." Then I explained my concerns and whom I wanted to ring up. She agreed to let me use the telephone and helped make the call. Walking back to the classroom, I felt pounds lighter. As Clem had warned, you can't let things go too long before turning them around.

But my glee lasted only a few moments. I spied Esteban up the hall and hoped for a nice little chat. So I walked over, smiling brightly. But as I neared, his menacing expression wiped the smile off my face. "What…what's wrong?" I asked.

"My auntie, Consuela Lopez, got some news," he said, scowling.

My knees suddenly felt weak, like I might topple over. "What…what is it?"

"Her son, Manuel, was in the New Mexico battalion. They all had to surrender to the Japanese, every soldier."

"Oh dear," I exclaimed.

"That's not the really bad part," Esteban said. "Once the Japanese soldiers were in charge, they forced the Americans to march miles and miles. Our guys had no food or water for days. The Japs killed anyone who couldn't walk fast enough. If a man slowed down, they stuck a bayonet in his ribs. "

"Oh my God," I gasped. "Did Manuel escape?"

"He was shot and left for dead. Some Filipino peasants found him and saved his life. But he's still in bad shape, really bad."

"What…what about the others?"

Esteban shook his head, his eyes dark with pain. "Many are dead, the rest are starving and tortured."

His grief exploded into bitter anger. He almost spit out the next words. "Those damn Japs. They're murderers. Murderers!" His eyes narrowed to slits. "But we're gonna get 'em! Tonight. Lots of people are angry. We're going over there! We're gonna get 'em."

Before I could even respond, he whipped around and rushed down the hall. On his way, he called to several buddies. They pressed close together and talked. Their fury heated the air around them.

154

I've rarely felt so ill. Not even during the ship's crossing, when the waves tossed us around and I turned green with nausea. The war had arrived—it was here, right across town. Esteban and the others were so angry they might break into the camp tonight. It would be dark and chaotic. They wouldn't know whom they attacked. I had seen the Japanese inmates; some were old, none had weapons to defend themselves. What if they killed somebody? What if they accidentally killed a kind, gentle person like…like Mr. Haiyoko? It wouldn't just be awful for the Japanese, it would be awful for Esteban and his pals.

I knew I had to tell somebody. And quick. I hurried back to the school office. But Mrs. Belfrey's office was empty. Only the new school secretary, Miss Gigi, was at her desk.

"Can I help you?" Miss Gigi asked sweetly. She had soft blue eyes and wavy, blond hair.

Somehow I couldn't imagine this pleasant, young woman dealing with a crowd of angry people. "Where's Mrs. Belfry?" I asked.

"She's substituting for Mr. Jeffers this afternoon. Then she has a meeting downtown with the superintendent. Is there any way I can help you?"

I shook my head and returned to the classroom. Five desks were empty at the back of the classroom. Esteban and his friends had left school early. For nearly two hours, I stared at the back of Francis's head. I knew he'd be leaving quickly. And I needed to speak to him first.

When the final bell rang, I sprang out of my desk. "Francis!" I called loudly.

He glanced back impatiently.

"Really, it's important," I insisted.

He paused, though clearly anxious to leave. When I told him what Esteban had said, however, his face turned white as the chalk lining the narrow shelf on the chalkboard behind him.

"Maybe you can tell your uncle," I exclaimed.

"My uncle?" His lip curled in disgust. "His name for the camp is Jap Trap. Says something ugly about 'em every day." He shook his head. "If there's a fight and a chance of someone getting bloodied, he won't want to miss it."

That silenced me. Now I understood why Francis was so unhappy living there, living with someone whose feelings were so different from his own.

"But you're going into the camp this afternoon, aren't you? Taking candy and stamps and stuff? You can tell Mr. Haiyoko."

Francis bit his lip, thinking hard. "Maybe, but it won't be enough. Who will believe him? Not the guards and they're the only ones who could stop this."

Of course he was right. Someone else needed to be told. Someone outside the camp, someone who wasn't Japanese. "I'll find someone to tell," I promised. "You go run your errand. At least you can warn the people inside."

He looked discouraged as he hurried off. And I understood why. How could the men inside defend themselves against an angry mob?

Seeing Arabella in the schoolyard, I started to run up and tell her. Then I spied a little smile on her lips and a dimple in her cheek. No wonder, she was chatting with Hank. How could I spoil one of her few pleasurable moments in recent weeks? So I kept moving.

156

Whom could I tell? Uncle Diego was head of our household, at present. He hated to be interrupted while painting. Still, as soon as I reached his studio, I knocked on the door. At first there was no answer. I knocked louder. Opening the door, Uncle Diego tried not to glare at me. "What is it, Beatrice? It better be important."

"It is, it is!" I exclaimed. But then I made a serious mistake. First I told him about the telephone call I had made that afternoon, though I didn't tell all. Nonetheless, his face turned red, his hand, grasping a paintbrush, shook with anger. "Oh Lord, Beatrice, That's none of your business! You're going to cause a lot of trouble over nothing!"

"It's not nothing, Uncle Diego," I responded indignantly. "Arabella is extremely unhappy." I tried to explain *how* unhappy but without mentioning the poison. If Lola learned of the poison, I knew she'd go nuts.

"Of course Arabella's upset. But she'll get over it. She always does." He started to close the door.

His indifference to his niece's feelings infuriated me, but then I remembered what I needed to say. "Please, I have something else to tell you." I exclaimed, gripping the door and trying to force it open. "Something urgent!

"Not today, Beatrice. You've caused me enough anxiety. My afternoon could be ruined. I won't be able to paint a thing!" Then he really did push me away and slam the studio door. I heard him bolt it shut.

It was nearly 4:00 p.m by now, and I was no closer to a solution. Who else could I speak to? I racked my brain. Miss White seemed like the most logical choice. She was a strong, sensible person who wasn't afraid to act. I dialed the number of El Delirio, and her secretary answered. "Miss White is traveling to Colorado Springs at present. She'll be back next week. Would you like to leave her a message?"

Saying no, I started to put down the phone. Then I had another idea. "How about Mr. Scott? Is he there?"

"I believe he is. I can ring him for you."

Since I had wanted to speak with Mr. Scott anyway, I was happy to reach him. But I decided not to mention Mr. Prestre first. I didn't want to divert him from the major problem at hand. I had already made that mistake with Uncle Diego. So I told him straight out what I'd heard from Esteban, though I just said "a school friend," not mentioning him by name. "Can you help?" I concluded.

He considered a moment. "Perhaps," he responded. "It's a nasty business and should be avoided."

Hanging up, I sighed with relief, certain Mr. Scott would do what he could.

Next, it seemed important to tell Francis. It would ease his mind and hopefully ease the minds of those inside. I rushed across town to his little house. When I knocked on the door, however, his uncle opened it. The large, rough-looking man almost filled the doorframe. And he didn't seem the least bit glad to see me.

"Whatcha' doing here?" he said sharply.

"I...I came to see Francis. We, uh, have a class project together and...and...." I stammered to a halt, unable to think of another word.

It didn't matter, because his uncle had no intention of letting me see Francis. "The boy's a nutcase. Up to no good. He had a simple job to do—selling stuff—but now he's telling secrets, too."

"Secrets?" I wondered what Mr. McKetchum had found out.

His eyes narrowed. "You ain't in on it too, are you?"

"In on what?" I endeavored to look innocent.

"Telling the Japs what they damn well don't need to know."

Oh dear. How had the uncle discovered what Francis was planning to do?

"No, no, I'm only here for a school project," I claimed loudly. "Couldn't I see him for a minute?"

"He doesn't need to be doing any school project. Not tonight. Not him. He's gonna stay in his room where he belongs."

"Yes, sir," I said. "I understand. I really do but...but perhaps I could speak with him for a tiny bit?" I gazed at the large man in the most endearing way possible. "So he won't worry about his grade. Just five minutes, please."

For an endless moment, Mr. McKetchum regarded me, his eyes narrowed. "Okay. Two minutes." He opened the door wide enough for me to squeeze past. "That's all you got."

I headed straight for Francis's room. I hoped Mr. McKetchum wouldn't notice that I knew the way. The door was locked from the outside with a bolt lock. I slid it open and rushed inside.

Francis was sitting forlornly on his bed. Again I was reminded of the stray dog in the alley, rummaging for scraps.

Seeing me, his expression didn't change. "He told you, I guess? What a fool I was, thinking my uncle might, might help...." His voice died out and he shook his head. "I was desperate, you see. But he'll never change. Never."

"Listen, please, I have good news. At least I hope so." I told him what Mr. Scott had said.

Francis looked a wee bit less gloomy. "Thanks, Beatrice."

"I didn't do it just for you," I responded quickly.

"I know." He shook his head again. "Still, I wanted to warn Mr. Haiyoko. I want him to be prepared. What if Mr. Scott doesn't get through in time? What if they don't give his message to the camp commander? It'll be terrible."

I knew he was right. "And there isn't any way you can leave here?"

"Are you kidding? I'm stuck." His eyes circled the small room and his shoulders sagged.

"Then I shall go!" The words just flew out of my mouth.

"What?" He looked at me doubtfully.

"You have candy and stamps and stuff?" I was thinking as I spoke.

He nodded. "Plenty." He pointed to a bag on the floor.

"Then I'll tell the guards in charge that I'm selling the stuff today. I'll say you're sick and couldn't come."

He stared at me as if I were mad. And, in fact, I felt a little mad. Why in the world did I say I would go?

But if I was a bit batty, Francis didn't mind in the least. He jumped off the bed and grabbed the bag from the floor. He explained what was in it: twenty packages of gum, fifteen packs of cigarettes, and three dozen stamps. "That's all I could manage to get. As soon as I can, I'll bring more. As soon as my uncle lets me go."

"Do you believe he *will* let you go?" I asked anxiously.

"He's too greedy not to," he said. "It's just tonight be-cause...because of the trouble. He doesn't want me telling anything to anybody."

He handed me the paper sack and I stuck it under my coat as the door swung open. "Your two minutes are up. That's enough time." I quickly left the room. Mr. McKetchum sneered, "That kid's not going anywhere tonight. I'll see to that." A strange smile crossed his face. "I'm a prison guard, ain't I? I know how to keep somebody locked up."

I practically ran out of the house and kept running. Half a block away, I paused to look down at the map that Francis had scribbled on the bag. It wasn't a very clear drawing, but I figured it would get me there. It was only half a mile from where I stood. Thank goodness the days were getting longer. With any luck, I could get there before dark.

CHAPTER TWENTY-SIX

I was halfway to the camp when I heard loud, angry voices. Twenty or more men and several women were standing near a bridge that crossed the Santa Fe River. Every person seemed to be carrying something: hatchets, a pitchfork, shotguns, shovels; one man even held a sword.

Carefully staying some distance away, I scanned the crowd for Esteban. But I didn't see him.

A plump woman with curly, black hair harangued the group. "You know how much fish they eat? Cans and cans of salmon and tuna. All they can stuff in their mouths."

A thin man with a reddish nose and bald head spoke next. "All they can eat, huh? My family's lucky to roast a chicken every few weeks."

A sturdy man with a shock of white hair struck his cane on the ground. "It ain't the fish or chicken we come here to talk about. It's how our boys are being treated in the Philippines."

The group fell silent. "The Japs are torturing, starving,

killing them," he said. "They don't deserve decent treatment when they are being so cruel, so ungodly to our sons."

The crowd loudly mumbled its agreement. One young man spoke up. "When are we gonna go get 'em? We should go now!"

The older man shook his head. "There's only twenty or so of us here now. The guards could easily stop us. More people are on their way. When we get forty or fifty, we'll head over."

At those words, I moved away and started running again. I didn't have much time. I needed to reach the camp before they did. Departing, I spied Esteban heading toward the crowd. He was accompanied by several close friends. Each had some sort of weapon. I glimpsed the blade of a knife gleaming in Esteban's hand.

I ran faster, hardly able to catch my breath. Then I paused, unsure of the direction. I peered at the map, but by now it was too dim for me to see clearly. I hated to ask anyone, but I didn't dare lose my way. A pregnant woman passed nearby, toting two heavy shopping bags. "Excuse me, ma'am," I called to her. "Do you know where the camp is?"

She put down her bags and gazed at me sharply. "What camp?"

"The old army camp."

She shrugged and pointed. "Over there, I think. Not far." She picked up her bags and trudged on. I ran in the direction she'd pointed. After a few minutes, I could see lights and a tall fence topped by barbed wire. By the time I reached the gate, I was gasping for air. A guard manned the entry. "Halt," he commanded. "No one allowed in."

"But…but I've brought stuff—gum and stamps and stuff–

for the men inside," I stammered. "Francis usually brings it, but he couldn't tonight."

"Who's Francis?"

"He…he's a friend of mine."

The guard studied me closer. "What's your name? How old are you?" He was trying not to smile.

I pulled myself upright. "My name is Beatrice Agatha Sims, and I'm thirteen years old, if you must know."

"Hmm, any ID to prove it?" he asked.

I realized he wasn't much older than I. All of eighteen, with a buzz haircut and big ears that stuck out from his head. "No, I didn't bring any." I hadn't imagined being asked for identification. And I wasn't sure what I could have brought— maybe my passport.

The guard appeared to check a notebook in front of him. "No deliveries expected." He snickered, "Certainly, not from a thirteen-year-old girl named Beatrice."

I could feel my cheeks flaming. How impudent he was!

"I insist on seeing the person in charge," I demanded. "I'm here for an important purpose and I don't like being ignored."

"Oh, you don't, huh?" His voice was still insolent. But I must have impressed him, because he picked up a phone. "I'd like to speak to the chief officer, please. There's a young lady here *claiming* she has important business and needs to be admitted." He listened a moment and then turned to me, a bit apologetic. "Sorry. The chief is at dinner."

I stared back at him a second, desperately thinking what to do. I couldn't take no for an answer. I needed gumption and plenty of it.

Steeling myself, I stood as erect as possible. Then with the imperious tone Great-Aunt Augusta used in demanding someone do something, I spoke. "Call back, tell them I need to see the chief officer immediately. Immediately. It's absolutely essential—a matter of life and death." I let my eyes bore into the young man. "And if you don't act this very instant..." I didn't need to finish the threat for this time the young man jumped into action. He picked up the phone and made a brief, urgent call, and then looked at me. "Hold on. Someone's coming to get you."

A few minutes later, another young man arrived and escorted me to the chief's office. Pacing back and forth, I kept glancing at the clock on the wall. Thirty-five minutes had passed since I saw the crowd near the bridge.

Finally the official in charge of the camp entered the room, still carrying his cloth napkin from dinner. His thoughtful manner and horn-rimmed glasses reminded me of my father. Plus, he listened to me in a serious, respectful way.

"I received a call earlier today," he said, observing me gravely. "Did you have something to do with that?"

"Mr. Scott?"

He nodded. "I had hoped it was a rumor and that nothing would develop. But it seems like it has."

From outside, we began hearing shouts and angry voices. The commander frowned and then cautioned me, "You stay here—right in this room—until I return. Understand?"

I nodded as he quickly walked out. I had no intention of going anywhere, anyway. Though I was almost less fearful of the crowd than I was of Esteban. If he spotted me, what might he think? I hated to even guess.

I stationed myself behind a curtain at the window and

gazed out. The commander stood in front of the entrance, accompanied by several guards with rifles. The crowd had grown to fifty or sixty people, all sorts of people. I recognized a few: a grocer, a mechanic, even a printer and a postman. I guessed they were all reasonable people who had become extremely distraught over the recent bad news. Upset to the point where they felt they had to take action.

The chief official also understood their feelings. He spoke clearly over a megaphone. "We don't know everything that's going on in the Philippines. But I know people are hearing some pretty terrible things."

The noise of the crowd swelled. A woman's voice yelled out loudly, "They're our boys. Our boys. They're killing our boys."

The chief responded quickly. "You deserve to be angry. I'm angry. But we can't respond viciously, with vengeance— an eye for an eye and a tooth for a tooth. We must behave as Americans. We must treat others fairly and decently. It's our duty as citizens of this country."

The clamor rose again, almost drowning out the commander. But again his voice resounded through the megaphone. "Over one hundred thousand Japanese people have been put in camps in the United States in recent months. You must understand they are *not* prisoners of war. They never took part in this war. Many of them are American citizens. They are being held in camps like this one for their safety and for any potential threat they pose to this country. But they have not been convicted of any crime; they have not borne arms against the United States. To harm them in any way would be against every principle our country holds dear. Most important, our behavior toward them can and will be held up as the standard. If we want other countries to abide by these standards, we need to set a good example, an honorable example."

His words had a quieting effect on the group. A few continued to grumble and shout. But gradually, people began to peel off in twos and threes. They walked off in different directions. Heading home, I figured. Home to sons and daughters and wives—to other worried and frightened people.

Though watching carefully, I didn't see Esteban.

Finally, the chief official returned to the office and sank into a chair. He barely seemed to notice I was still in the room.

"You were very brave, sir," I ventured at last. He looked up. "No, you were very brave. I am an official of the United States government. It is my responsibility to keep the Japanese men staying here safe." He smiled slightly. "Why did *you* think it was so important to come?"

"I'm not sure, sir." I considered a moment. "I just didn't think it was fair. To attack unarmed men."

He sighed. "I wish everyone in the world agreed with you."

"I was in London, sir, when bombs dropped out of the sky," I added, feeling tears in my voice. "I thought...how could they possibly drop bombs on us? We're not soldiers. We're innocent people."

The chief official didn't answer for a moment. "You did me a favor warning me. Is there anything I can do for you before you head home?"

An idea popped into my head. "There's someone I'd like to speak to. Just for a minute, please."

Indeed, I only had to wait a short while. A young guard entered, accompanied by an elderly man, dressed simply in

168

loose, gray clothes.

"Mr. Haiyoko?" I said shyly.

He nodded with a tiny smile and then pressed the palms of his hands together and bowed slightly. "Do you know me?"

"Well, in a way I do," I exclaimed. "Francis, you see, is very fond of you."

"Oh yes, Francis." His smile grew. "And I'm very fond of him—a fine boy. Where is he tonight? I was expecting to see him." Mr. Haiyoko looked concerned. His eyes were dark and grave, as if they saw widely and understood deeply.

"His uncle is…keeping him inside for a while," I explained. "But you'll see him soon. He is planning to bring you some drawings."

"I look forward to that. And seeing you, too, perhaps." He gave another small bow and left with the guard.

Minutes later, I was fairly skipping out the gates. So pleased, so relieved. Nothing terrible had happened. No one had been hurt. I could report to Francis that Mr. Haiyoko and the other men were safe. At least for the present.

I was so carefree, in fact, that I nearly ran into someone before recognizing his familiar face. "I thought that was you," said Esteban. "What were you doing in the camp?" His voice was harsh, unfriendly.

I wasn't sure what to say. I didn't want to lie, but I dreaded telling him what I had done. I stammered, "I…I went to see Mr. Haiyoko."

"Who?" demanded Esteban.

"He's a friend, I mean he's a…a friend of a friend."

"But I told you this afternoon there was going to be trouble." His eyes looked black in the dim light. "You didn't tell Mr.

Ha-Haiku what I said? You didn't warn him, did you?"

I shook my head. "I didn't, I promise. I just…I just spoke to him for a few minutes. Then he said goodbye and bowed."

"Bowed? To you?" Esteban frowned. "That's really dumb. I can't believe you'd go in there. Or talk to any of those Japs."

But I could tell that he was already less upset. The two of us started walking back toward our homes. "My goodness, Esteban," I exclaimed. "Mr. Haiyoko is an old man. Like your Uncle Nogales. He's never hurt anyone, I'm sure. He doesn't deserve to be hurt." Too late I realized what had slipped out.

"Hurt? You think I'd hurt an old man?" Even in the dark, I could see the pain in his face that I'd even think such a thing about him.

"I…I wasn't sure."

He fell silent for a long moment. I wondered if he'd speak again but finally he did. "I heard what that man said—the one in charge. And it made sense." His voice trembled. "But…but what if Manuel doesn't make it back? Or Ricardo? What if I never see my cousins again?"

I reached out and put my hand on his arm. What could I say? Nothing. There was nothing to say. The war was barely beginning for those in the United States and yet it had already created so much misery. Oh, how I longed for it to finish soon.

The two of us walked the rest of the way in silence. But I felt that Esteban was more sad now than angry. In fact, when we reached the Plaza, he paused. "Would you like me to walk with you all the way?" he said. "Seeing as it's so dark and all."

"Thank you." I smiled a bit. "That's very chivalrous of you. But it's only a few blocks. And not that late." Actually, a number of people were still out, enjoying the balmy April air.

The newsboy was hawking the evening paper. A couple near us was laughing. And music floated from La Fonda Hotel on the corner. Inside, probably dozens of people were dancing to the band without a clue of what had happened a mere mile away.

So after saying goodnight, the two of us headed in our different directions. At first, I felt immensely relieved, almost lightheaded. A few minutes later, however, I began to worry. I had dodged telling Esteban the whole truth about going to the camp. I had feared losing his friendship. But now I felt I had been dishonest. Even if he didn't learn everything that had happened tonight, it would always color our friendship.

Almost the instant I opened the door to Arabella's house, however, my worries vanished. A fragrant aroma filled my nostrils. My goodness, I was starving! I'd forgotten about food until that very moment. Now I couldn't wait another second. Hurrying into the kitchen, I glimpsed Arabella at the stove waving a wooden spoon like a fairy's wand over a simmering pan of red tomato sauce. The giant spaghetti pot bubbled on the next burner.

"Did you fry a pork chop on the bottom?" I asked while fetching plates and silverware."

She pointed to Stanley's recipe next to the stove, declaring, "Of course I did." Then she exclaimed, "And I have news! Big news!"

"Well, tell me over dinner," I said forking up a giant pile of spaghetti and spooning sauce on top.

Arabella plopped down opposite me at the table. Her plate was filled as well. But before taking a bite, she blurted out, "I'm leaving."

"What?" My fork stopped midway to my mouth. "Leaving Santa Fe?"

She nodded vigorously. "Today Uncle Diego received a telephone call from Ariadne. She's sending me tickets to Cleveland."

"Why, that's wonderful!" Without thinking, I jerked my fork. A blob of tomato sauce flew across the table. "Wonderful!"

"Gosh," Arabella sighed with relief. "I was so afraid you'd be upset."

"Oh no," I put down my fork and came around the table to hug her. "You know how much I want to be with my family, don't you?" She nodded. I squeezed her. "So, naturally, I'm thrilled you can be with yours."

"She often promised. But this is the *first* time, really the first time, she's sending tickets," exclaimed Arabella. "They'll arrive at the Western Union office tomorrow." She sounded perplexed. "I can't imagine why she decided that I must come right now. Can you?"

"It doesn't matter *why*," I replied, concealing a tiny smile. "Let's simply rejoice that she did decide now was the time to ask you." And thank goodness she did, I thought.

I returned to my seat and we both plowed into our spaghetti. Between mouthfuls, Arabella told me about the grand house Ariadne and Stanley had rented in Cleveland. How it had a large kitchen where Stanley and she could spend hours cooking. "Won't that be heaven!" she gasped. Plus, the house had a living room, library, porch, and several bedrooms.

She hesitated, "Did you hear what I said? Three or four bedrooms? Why don't you come with me? We can each have our own room."

I shook my head. "I need to stay in Santa Fe for now. But that's kind of you to ask."

I looked around. "I can't stay *here*, of course. But I'll figure out something." My gaze returned to my best friend. Her face was pink with happiness. "I'm so pleased things turned out well. I believe you and your mother and Stanley will have an extraordinary time together."

It did seem like a fairy-tale ending to a story that could have had a much, much darker conclusion. And what if I had added a bit of fairy dust to make it happen? Sometimes, that's what's needed.

All at once, my head felt extremely heavy, as if it might drop into my nearly empty spaghetti dish. In fact, my entire body ached as though I'd run to the moon and back. Indeed, it seemed as if that day I had traveled a much greater distance than ever, ever before.

CHAPTER TWENTY-SEVEN

The ring of the telephone awakened me the next morning. Somehow I guessed it was for me. And I managed to pick it up by the seventh ring.

"Hello," I said into the receiver.

"Hallo, I b'lieve 'tis the very lass I was hoping to speak to. Is that so, Beatrice?" How cheery to hear Mr. Scott's warm voice. "How are you doing this bright shiny morning?"

"Fine, I believe. I'm just waking up."

"No doubt, you deserved a very good sleep last night. A very good sleep, indeed. After all you did yesterday."

I wasn't quite sure how to reply, so he continued.

"I checked in with the captain at the internment camp first thing this morning and got a report on the goings-on last night. A bad business, it was. Fortunately, they were well warned. First by me, and then, it appears, by you."

"Yes, I'm afraid I did stop by for a short visit with the chief of the camp," I responded.

"Afraid? Fear has no place in what you did," he explained. "You were a brave lass, you were. Very brave. You and your family have much to be proud of. I will certainly let them know."

"Thank you," I said with such a magnificent smile that I thought he might feel it through the phone lines. Just then, however, the image of Mr. Prestre loomed up in my mind. "There's something else I need to speak to you about," I hastened to say, eager to satisfy my curiosity about that sinister figure. "Could we meet somewhere today?"

"Why, I was going to suggest the very same thing," said Mr. Scott. "Do you know of Miss White's tearoom? Why don't I treat you to a cup of fine British tea and some biscuits as soon as you're out of school today?"

Nothing could have pleased me more, and I said so. Then I rushed to get ready for school. I looked forward to speaking with Francis. I was less eager to see Esteban.

First thing, I told Francis that the camp had been warned and the disastrous attack averted. The poor boy wiped away tears of relief. Then he surprised both of us by grasping me in a quick, awkward hug.

"Uncle let me out. I knew he would. So this afternoon I'm buying more gum and stamps," he exclaimed, his eyes shining. "And I plan to bring Mr. Haiyoko a drawing pencil and colored chalks and a pad of paper. That will keep him busy."

Later that day, I glanced over at Francis, seated at his desk. He was certainly an odd fellow. But he had been worth the bother to get to know. And, perhaps, through him, I might spend some time with Mr. Haiyoko. That might prove interesting.

School had ended before I could manage to speak to Esteban. Seeing him in the schoolyard, I hurried over. He gazed at me earnestly. And I returned the look as openly as possible, unafraid for once to reveal my heart's true feelings, and hoping he'd recall those tender feelings, whatever he might think of me after what I had to say.

Then I spoke quickly, not wishing to lose courage. "What I told you last night, Esteban, wasn't exactly true. I did speak to Mr. Haiyoko but...." My voice almost failed me. I glanced down at my hands, which were shaking. Then I took another breath, steeled myself, and looked up. "But before that, I met with the camp's chief. And...and I did warn him."

The warmth in Esteban's gaze faded. For a moment he didn't speak, and then he muttered, "Yeah, I kinda figured you did." He stood still another second, staring at me, then turned, and started walking away.

"So what do you think?" I called after him. "Are you sorry you trusted me?"

He paused, glancing back. "I'm not sure. I'm not sure what I think." He shook his head and continued walking, a little slouched, his hands stuck deep in his pockets. A friend yelled at him but he kept moving.

Oh dear, I clasped my hands tightly together, why did I believe I must tell him the whole truth? What if I lost his friendship? In a few days, Arabella would be leaving town. Who knew when I'd see her again, if ever? And now I might lose Esteban, as well. I could hardly bear the thought.

For the first time in my life I wanted to *mope* like Arabella sometimes did—just crawl into bed, put the covers over my head, fall asleep, and hope that when I awoke...either I or the world would be different.

Yet, instead, somehow my feet carried me downtown to Miss White's tea shop. Mr. Scott was already seated with a teapot, creamer, sugar bowl and a plate full of biscuits. He looked up cheerfully. "Why, hallo, lass."

I couldn't even reply, my thoughts were so muddled. I sank into the chair. "Please, tell me what's on your mind," he said gently.

So I told him everything, start to finish. He sat thoughtfully a moment and then took my hand and held it. "I'm afraid, dear lass, that's how a war treats people. It makes them choose sides, not only on the battlefront, but everywhere. One person pitted against another. It's the same in this little town as anywhere else."

He let go of my hand and poured me a cup of hot tea. "Cream?" I nodded, and he added a generous amount of cream. "Sugar?"

I nodded again, and he added several teaspoons of sugar. "Drink up, lassie. Nothing heals the soul like a pot of fresh tea." Indeed, I did sip the tea slowly, and it was very soothing.

"It's possible your friend will understand in time. The war is likely to be hard on everyone for the news is going to get a lot worse before it's better. And the fighting could last much longer than anyone expects." Mr. Scott looked directly into my eyes. "But trust that you did the right thing and let it sort itself out. That's all a body can do sometimes."

I sat silent a moment, considering what he'd said. Perhaps there was no more to be done at present. I must simply wait and hope things turned out well. I looked into Mr. Scott's kind face, grateful for the bit of solace he was offering. I knew there was something else I had wanted to consult him about. But what was it? It took a moment to recall. Then I remembered Mr. Prestre. "It may sound silly," I murmured. "But I feel compelled to tell you about another possible danger, right here in Santa Fe."

"What's that, lass?" His eyes gleamed mischievously. "You seem to know all the goings-on in town."

"Do you know a person named Mr. Prestre? He spoke to you at the dog examination. He says he's Swiss." For a second, I wondered if that was the name he had used with Mr. Scott. Or if he had assumed some sort of alias, as Arabella had suggested.

But he responded quickly, "James Prestre? He *is* Swiss—a Swiss hunting guide. Claims he's been all over the world on hunting expeditions, killed tigers and such. Though he seems to have settled in Santa Fe for the present. Damn fool that he is."

"A hunter? So he was telling me the truth about why he was up in the hills above the city," I said, adding. "The day I stayed with the dogs."

"He was there then?" Mr. Scott stared at me quizzically.

I nodded. "He left when you arrived with the vet." But that explained only *one* location where I had seen Mr. Prestre. Was there also a reason he was present at the train station when the Japanese arrived? And at the Dogs for Defense examination? It seemed bizarre that our paths had so often crossed. And yet perhaps it was simply a coincidence. Santa Fe was, after all, a very small town.

"You just said he was a fool, Mr. Scott," I said. "Why is that?"

"Oh my goodness, Prestre has been trying to convince me of the most idiotic scheme. He wants to use my dogs to track down Japanese people on the battlefield," he explained. "Prestre thinks it would be possible to train dogs to sniff out different races of people—those that are now the enemy—and attack them."

It was my turn to stare at him. "Attack them? Attack the Japanese in particular?"

"I told him it was the most preposterous thing I'd ever heard." Mr. Scott shook his head. "Furthermore, I'd never waste my dogs' precious time on something as outrageous as that."

He began to laugh. "But the idiot wouldn't give up the dumb idea. Said he was going to take it straight to Congress and the president. Maybe he will do just that. Then they'll discover it's a big waste of time, too."

I had to smile a bit too—at myself. All my fears and worries about Mr. Prestre, the spy, had also been a big waste of time. Thank goodness, I hadn't confessed everything to Mr. Scott. He might think me quite foolish as well. And yet, in another way, I felt that Mr. Prestre was still a dangerous man. If people believed his crazy notions…a shiver ran through me. That was too horrid to contemplate.

We had both finished our tea by now. But I dallied a little longer. It was so reassuring to be with the hearty Scotsman. And I didn't relish the possibility of returning to Arabella's house. She was probably packing to leave, cheerful as could be. Meanwhile, Uncle Diego would be in a foul mood. He loved his niece and hated to lose her company. As for Lola—well, she was never any comfort.

Fortunately, as I stood and gathered my things, Mr. Scott spoke again. "I have to say I've saddled myself with a rather heavy load. And I hardly know how to manage."

"Why, what is that?"

"How am I going to care for all the fine pups my Zara is going to have in a week or so—ten or twelve, by the look of her? While at the same time, I've got to train a batch of new dogs for the military." He shook his head. "Who's gonna brush and feed the wolfhounds and make sure the puppies get the attention they need?"

He stroked his chin as if hard in thought. "I've got to find somebody reliable and kind and who's very fond of dogs. Also she or he needs to be very close by, willing to pitch in at a moment's notice."

"My goodness, you really do need someone." My voice almost failed me. Suddenly the solution to my dilemma appeared quite simple and obvious. I spoke more strongly, "When does Miss White return?"

He gave me a keen look. "In a day or two at the most, I believe."

"Do you mind asking her to ring me up immediately? I have a question for her, an important question. And I...I'm looking forward to the answer."

He nodded firmly, with a bit of a twinkle in his eyes, assuring me it would be no problem. Then he put a hand on my shoulder. "You've done quite a lot on your own for a lass your age," he said.

"But I didn't want to," I hastened to reply. "I didn't want to do so much on my own, without Clem or anyone helping me out."

He shook his head gravely. "None of us do. That's one of the hardest bits about growing up. Understanding what needs to be done and then gathering the strength and courage to do it. But sooner or later you come 'round to it. And often it's better sooner than later."

After leaving the tearoom, I walked up Palace Avenue on my own. The street and the houses looked a good deal more cheerful than earlier in the afternoon when I had headed towards town. Indeed, it seemed the world and my life were filled with changes. Some a good deal more pleasant than others. Yet the last few months hadn't been altogether awful. It had required a dreadful incident to pull the United States into the war. But now my country, Great Britain, had a huge and powerful partner. Surely, together, the two nations and their allies would be victorious. And I would finally be able to return home to my beloved family.

But who would return? A very different sort of Beatrice, for sure. A girl my family might barely recognize. I had been challenged in ways that would have been unimaginable only a short time ago when I was a very protected and pampered English girl. And yet I hadn't backed down or been defeated, not once. What was ahead? Would I visit Arabella in Cleveland? Would Clem ever return to Santa Fe? And would Esteban and I become friends again as before, especially dear friends? I hoped so—oh, I did hope so.

And yet, quite honestly, there was no way to know what lay ahead. There were bound to be changes I couldn't foresee. For a second my step faltered and my gaze dropped. I reached out to steady myself on the adobe wall bordering the sidewalk.

Then I noticed a giant lilac bush straight ahead. It was covered with tight buds, soon to burst open into fragrant purple blooms. My gaze lifted. My spirit was seized, as it often was in Santa Fe, by the freshness of the air, the blueness of the sky and the brightness of the clear light.

Why not view the unknown future in a different manner? Not as frightening and overwhelming but as a bit exciting. How thrilling *not* to know everything that was going to happen next! I only needed to possess the gumption to face whatever arrived —certain any upcoming adventures would be as remarkable as the last.

AUTHOR'S NOTES

Beatrice is a fictional story based on true events.

Early in the morning of December 7, 1941 Japanese war-planes appeared in the skies over Pearl Harbor, an American naval port on the island of Oahu, in Hawaii. The Japanese warplanes dropped thousands of bombs killing over 2,000 American soldiers, sailors, and civilians. A day later the United States declared war on Japan and the day after that Japan's ally, Nazi Germany, declared war on the United States.

In the panic that followed, Americans feared attacks from Japan on cities along the Pacific coast. Some Americans believed that anyone of Japanese heritage could be dangerous because they might send secret information to Japan or sabotage the United States. Though not everyone agreed with this policy and a few protested it strongly, the U.S. government uprooted 110,000 Japanese-Americans living on the west coast. Men, woman and children were forced to leave their homes and businesses and farms. The Japanese-Americans were placed in internment camps throughout the west. Forty percent of the internees were American citizens; some had been born in the United States.

In Santa Fe, an internment camp was built at the site of an old army camp on the edge of town. The inmates were all men, usually professionals like teachers, preachers or businessmen. They arrived on March 14th at night by train and were taken in trucks to the camp. The camp remained in operation for the duration of the war. In general the Japanese men interned in Santa Fe were treated decently. They organized their own newspaper, sports teams and garden. At least one was an artist.

In August 1941, the New Mexico 200th and 515th Artillery Battalion had been posted to the Philippines, in the western Pacific. When Pearl Harbor was being attacked in Hawaii, the Japanese Imperial Army also attacked American military posts in the Philippines. After three months of heavy fighting in early April, the NM Battalion and other soldiers were forced to surrender. These soldiers became Japanese POWs (prisoners of war). The POWs were forced to march 65 miles without food or water up the Bataan Peninsula to POW camps. Many were were killed or died on route and the march became known as the Bataan Death March. Out of the 1800 New Mexico soldiers in the 200th Artillery Battalion only 900 survived the war.

In January, 1942 a national program was developed called Dogs for Defense. The United States Army was requesting dog-owners to relinquish their pets to serve in the military. Thousands of people came forth to give up their dogs. In Santa Fe, Amelia Elizabeth White, a prominent and well-respected member of the community, was in charge of the Dogs for Defense Program. Prior to the war, Ms. White and her sister raised Irish wolfhounds and Afghans for dog shows with the help of her trainer, Alex Scott, from Scotland. Ms. White lived in a beautiful spacious home known as El Delirio.

A Swiss game hunter named James Prestre believed that

it would be possible to train dogs to track people of Japanese heritage. He tried to convince the U.S. Military of this idea. An effort was made to train dogs for this purpose on Cat Island, off the coast of Alabama (see The History Detectives). Prestre lived in Santa Fe for a short time during the war years. The Army determined that his idea was a total failure.

Jerry R. West, Japanese Internment Camp, 2009, oil on canvas, 42 x 46 in. Collection of the New Mexico Museum of Art. Gift of Meridel Rubenstein, 2011 (2011.5) Photo by Blair Clark © Jerry R. West

The painting by Mr. West served as an inspiration for Odessa's cover illustration for *Beatrice On Her Own*.

Acknowledgements

I want to acknowledge the help I received from the Santa Fe Public Library; from Jean Schaumberg for her gracious introduction to the School of American Research which was formerly El Deliro, home of Amelia Elizabeth White; and, especially, to Nancy Owens Lewis whose research on Santa Fe's dogs for defense was invaluable to this story. I also relied on *The Silent Voices of WWII* by Nancy Bartlit for information about New Mexico soldiers in the Philippines and the Japanese Internment Camp in Santa Fe.

About the Author

Rosemary Zibart is a former journalist, author and playwright. She splits her time between Santa Fe where she lives with her family and a home in the countryside where she writes. She loves to hear from readers. Please contact her through her website www.rosemaryzibart.com or friend her on Facebook.